THE CURTAINED SLEEP

The Mull of Kintyre
contrasting strangely
is the thin borderline
a car-crash victim -
neurological institute
one of overwhelming
memory of his acc
undercurrents in the li   him while he
convalesces at a friend's home.

From being only marginally interested in their problems, he becomes totally involved in his friend's life in a truly horrifying way and suddenly has to face the possibility of his own imminent destruction mentally and physically.

ARCHIE ROY

Archie Roy is a Professor of Astronomy in the University of Glasgow. He is a Fellow of the Royal Astronomical Society, the Royal Society of Edinburgh and the British Interplanetary Society, a member of the International Astronomical Union and the Society for Psychical Research.

He conducts research in astrodynamics, celestial mechanics, astroarchaeology, parapsychology and mathematical models of the human memory. He has published 12 books, over 70 scientific papers and scores of articles in journals and magazines. Several of his books have been published in the United States, France, Russia and India. In a varied career he has travelled widely and lectured in many countries, been an invited speaker for NATO Scientific Division, edited journals and newspapers, investigated haunted houses and haunted people.

The publication of the British Public Lending Rights figures put him among the top ten per cent of novelists borrowed from libraries in the United Kingdom.

BY THE SAME AUTHOR

FICTION:

Deadlight
The Curtained Sleep
All Evil Shed Away
Sable Night
The Dark Host
Devil In The Darkness

NON–FICTION

Great Moments In Astronomy
Collins Larousse Encyclopedia Of Astronautics
(English Edition)
The Foundations of Astrodynamics
Astronomy: Principles and Practice
(co–author David Clarke)
Astronomy: Structure of the Universe
(co-author David Clarke)
Orbital Motion

THE CURTAINED SLEEP

ARCHIE ROY

Thanks & best wishes,
Archie Roy

Apogee

APOGEE BOOKS,
P.O. Box 230,
Glasgow G12 9EX
United Kingdom.

First published in Great Britain by John Long, London, 1969
This edition 1986
ISBN 1 869935 00 4

Made and printed in Great Britain by
William Collins Sons & Co, Ltd, Glasgow

For Ann and Alistair,
in memory of a lost weekend
and a day that made up for it

'and wicked dreams abuse the curtain'd sleep'.
Macbeth, ACT II, SCENE I

'The world becomes a dream and the dream becomes a world.' *Novalis*

I apologise to the inhabitants of the Mull of Kintyre for taking some slight liberty with their coastline. Although marked on the map, Port Mean as depicted here does not exist, nor does any character in this book. The events, nevertheless, while also fictitious, are quite consistent with our present-day knowledge of the human brain.

Glasgow

A.E.R.

Contents

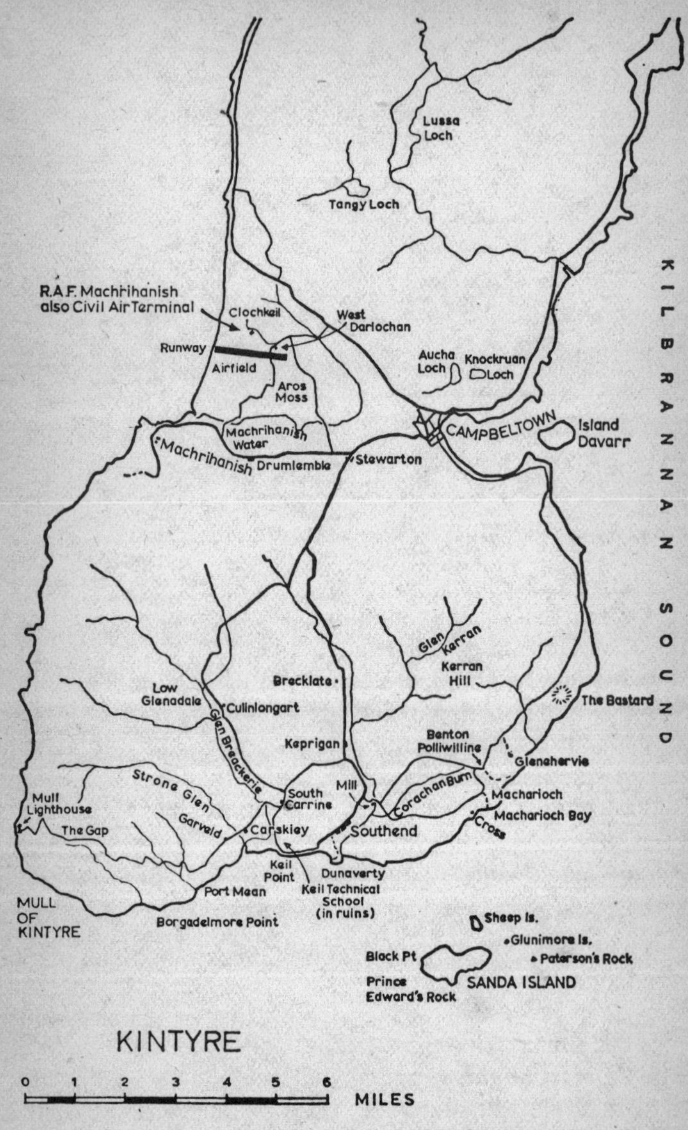
R.A.F. Machrihanish also Civil Air Terminal
Lussa Loch
Tangy Loch
Clochkeil
West Darlochan
Runway
Airfield
Aros Moss
Aucha Loch
Knockruan Loch
KILBRANNAN SOUND
Machrihanish Water
CAMPBELTOWN
Island Davarr
Machrihanish
Drumlemble
Stewarton
Glen Kerran
Kerran Hill
Brecklate
Low Glenadale
Culinlongart
Glen Breackerie
The Bastard
Keprigan
Benton
Polliwilline
Glenahervie
Strone Glen
Mill
Corachan Burn
Mull Lighthouse
South Carrine
Macharioch
Garveld
Machariooh Bay
The Gap
Carskiey
Southend
Cross
Keil Point
Dunaverty
Port Mean
Keil Technical School (in ruins)
MULL OF KINTYRE
Borgadelmore Point
Sheep Is.
Glunimore Is.
Black Pt
Paterson's Rock
Prince Edward's Rock
SANDA ISLAND
KINTYRE
0 1 2 3 4 5 6 MILES

Book one Largo

1 First awakening

Blackness. Blackness shot with dull red pain. Eyelids open. My eyelids. Head hurts. I am . . . Alan Ramsay. Hold on to that. Alan Ramsay. In bed. Cool, crisp linen tight about me.

Where am I? The pale blue ceiling tells me nothing. Silence, deep and soft-wrapping as a fleece. I turn my head slowly. A foot beyond the pillow stands a white, plastic-topped bedside locker. There is a glass jug of water and a tumbler on top of it. I try to raise my head. Fire scorches my brain; my head falls back, my ash-dry mouth gasping open. It is some time before I try again.

I turn my head very carefully to the left. The room is small. There is a wooden chair beside the bed. Beyond the window, the lime-green slats of its Venetian blind cutting down the sunlight's glare, is a cream-hued wall with a fitted wardrobe. I recognise nothing.

It is peaceful.

I raise my head once more. This time the pain is less severe. The door is closed. Now I notice above the bed a panel with switches and a push-button. There is a set of earphones hanging over the black metal bar at the head of the bed.

A hospital bed. I'm in a hospital. Why? I try to force the film of memory through the jammed projector of my mind and merely succeed in torturing my brain. I stop, willing relaxation. Everything melts away in mist. When I become conscious once more, the pain is duller, at the level of a moderately-severe headache, the light through the Venetian blind has faded, my mental faculties are less garish and tattered.

I must have lain quietly for some time until the utter stillness was broken by the distant peremptory barking of a dog. I dragged an arm from under the imprisoning sheets and sought the bell-push above my head. An unfamiliar grey-blue sleeve fell back from my wrist. After I had pressed the bell, I explored my attire, cautiously moving my limbs. I was in pyjamas. My left leg and my ankle hurt as well as my head. When I touched the side of my head I felt a gauze patch secured by Elastoplast or something similar.

The door opened. A girl in nurse's uniform entered, the stiff white apron over her dark blue wrapper whispering as she approached the bedside. Her fingers touched my wrist.

'Good,' she said quietly. 'How are you feeling?'

'Confused and sore. Where am I? What happened?'

'You've had an accident. But everything's going to be all right. Now just rest quietly and I'll tell Dr Selkirk you're awake.'

When she had gone, I tried to recall the circumstances of the accident without success. I was still trying when the door opened again. This time the nurse was accompanied by a young woman in a white coat. The nurse halted at the foot of the bed; the woman came to the bedside. Her head tilted forward, she examined my face. As I looked up, I couldn't help noting, even in my under-par state, the thick, close-cut dark hair, the oval, attractive face with steady, hazel eyes, the straight nose and warm mouth, the lower lip pleasantly full. She smiled genuinely.

'You've got a hard head. Do you feel up to answering some silly questions?'

'Yes.'

'Good. I am Dr Selkirk. You're in the David Campbell Neurological Institute.' She drew up a chair and sat down. 'You've had an accident and were brought here just before lunch today. Now: do you remember who you are?'

'Yes. Alan Ramsay, twenty-eight, address fifteen Huntly Terrace, Glasgow, W.2.'

'Excellent. Can you open your eyes wide?' I did so and the steady hazel eyes held mine. She seemed satisfied and nodded. 'Now. What is the last thing you remember?'

Quite suddenly an event—having coffee in the George Hotel in Inveraray—surfaced above the threshold. As if it was a knot on a piece of string I seized it and tugged. Other memory knots appeared. As I spoke, Dr. Selkirk's calm face reflected her attention.

'I was driving down here from Glasgow to the Department Outstation at Low Glenadale. I remember stopping for coffee in Inveraray. I remember passing through Lochgilphead—I got petrol there—and I remember going through Tarbet and Ballochroy.' I paused. 'But nothing after that.' I licked my lips. 'Nothing at all.'

She smiled reassuringly.

'Don't worry. You've had quite a knock on the head—there's probably mild concussion; in such cases the memories just prior to the accident are often lost. It's called retrograde amnesia. I wouldn't try to recall them. You'll find they'll come back by themselves.'

'But what happened?'

'For some reason you put your car into the hedge near Keprigan. You were brought here since it was nearest. We've X-rayed you and patched you up—there's nothing broken as far as we can see but you cut your head. I've put a few stitches in it.' She smiled again. 'I'm afraid we had to shave your head in that area.'

I asked about my car.

'It doesn't seem badly damaged. It was towed into Southend. You'll probably have a visit from the police but not before tomorrow. Nurse Macdonald here will look after you—you're probably thirsty.' I nodded then wished I hadn't. 'I'll look in again tomorrow morning to see you. Just try to sleep.' She rose to her feet.

'What's the time?'

'About five-thirty.'

'I must let Dr Black at the Outstation know what's happened. He was expecting me to arrive about twelve-thirty.'

She shook her head.

'It's all taken care of. We got your identity from your wallet and where you worked from your University diary. We phoned the Department of Geophysics. Your professor said he'd notify Dr Black and send someone down to take your place. He also said we weren't to let you go until we were sure you were all right.'

I relaxed, conscious that I wanted to sleep again.

She nodded.

'That's right. You'll feel much better in the morning.'

She left the room. I wondered vaguely what her first name was.

With Nurse Macdonald's surprisingly strong arm supporting my head, I swallowed some mouthfuls of cold water, its clean taste satisfying and all-sufficient. I lay back again and gazed at the ceiling. Apart from the dull head pain, I was aware of a feeling of tension, almost of alarm, all the more unpleasant because of my utter inability to put cause to it. I wondered if all accident victims felt this way, perhaps because of the hollow nothingness memory should have filled on command.

I drowsed.

Later that evening I was given a light meal also a sedative in the shape of a long green pill. Just before I fell asleep, while I was in that state where the sentry at the defences of the mind nods, something momentarily appeared through the misty opaqueness—a face, the face of someone I'd never seen before that day, a face warped with terror, mouth open, eyes staring. My heart thudded in resonant fear and I fought to fix the image but the mists closed in again. In spite of my effort to hold off sleep in case the mist cleared once more, my eyes closed on a memory as still as a deep-frozen pond.

. . . . .

Early morning sunlight wakened me. Even through the slats of the blind it seemed painfully bright, nevertheless I felt much better, my headache barely present. Soon after I opened my eyes, the night nurse stuck a thermometer into my armpit, nodded in satisfaction when she read the mercury level and brought me a basin and my own shaving things. While the shaving head of my electric razor droned to itself as it harvested my one-day growth ('in one day a man grows the equivalent of 400 inches of beard' the rag-bag of my mind informed me gratuitously) I tried to jolt more relevant pieces of information from my subconscious. But the computer store was still inaccessible and I turned to wondering if they'd let me go today. An hour and a half later a white-coated orderly brought my breakfast, consisting of porridge, milk, bacon and egg, toast and tea. I found I was reasonably hungry.

I had three visitors in quick succession after that, four if you count Dr Selkirk. The first was introduced by Nurse Macdonald.

'This is Constable Mckinnon. Do you feel well enough to speak to him?'

On being assured that I was, she bestowed a smile impartially on us and swept out of the door. The constable, a tall, fair-haired, well-built young man in his early twenties, sat down beside my bed, laid his peaked cap on the bedside table and fished out a notebook. He opened it and poised a pencil.

After the usual questions about who I was and where I lived and why I was going from A to B he came to the nub of the matter.

'Now then, sir, what do you remember about the accident?'

I paused but no memory came, only a nagging sense of frustration and apprehension. I raised my knees restlessly against the tug of the bedclothes.

'I'm sorry, Constable, I can't remember a thing.' I swallowed. 'I don't even remember passing through Campbeltown.'

'I see.' His pencil made marks on the page.

Alarm flooded through my body like water from a broken dam.

'Have you any idea what happened?' I spoke urgently, aware of a horrid possibility that they were perhaps keeping from me something nasty, perhaps that I had run over someone and killed them. My mouth burned and my stomach became chilled lead.

'Nothing to worry about, sir. There are one or two puzzling things but in the main we can see what happened. You were found unconscious in the driving seat of your car with the front of the car in the left hand hedge, the rear slewed across the road. From bloodstains, it appeared you banged your head when you went into the hedge.'

'But why should I swerve like that?' The edge of my tension was duller now.

'Ah, that we don't know, unless it was because you braked so suddenly. There were skidmarks in the road.'

'I jammed on the brakes?'

'Oh yes. Mind you, you weren't travelling all that fast—the length of the skidmarks tells us that. But it looks as if you swerved after you applied the brakes.'

I felt myself frowning. 'But that looks as if . . .'

'Yes, sir?'

'It looks as if I was trying to avoid something?'

'Yes, sir, it does, doesn't it?' He paused, regarding me thoughtfully. When I said nothing, he tried to jog my memory. 'And you have no recollection of the event?'

'Not the slightest.' My alarm had changed to bewilderment. If it had been another car, the driver would surely have stopped. I said as much to the policeman.

'Ah yes, but the road is straight there and although it's narrow, there's plenty of room for cars to pass. You'd have seen anyone coming a long way ahead. There'd've been plenty of time to steer your car to your side of the road even if you'd been driving on the crown.'

I leaned back against the propped-up pillows.

'Farm roads? Could anything have come out suddenly just in front of me?'

Mckinnon shook his head decisively. 'Nothing there, not for half a mile ahead on either side.' He got to his feet. 'Well, sir, I'll get on my way. I hope you're better soon. If you think of anything more, get in touch. Southend Police Station.' He paused at the door. 'By the way, your car is in Barker's Garage, Southend.'

I thanked him and he left. I had five minutes to worry fruitlessly over the situation before Nurse Macdonald poked her white-capped head round the door to inquire if I was fit enough for another visitor. I assured her I was so she stepped out of the way to allow a well-known but totally unexpected friend of mine to enter.

I hadn't seen Peter Campbell for five years or so but my first impression was that he hadn't changed. Just over average height, very slightly plump with dark wavy hair and a pleasant light-hearted expression, he wore a neat, rather expensive looking executive-grey business suit. His almost chubby face lit up with delight when he saw me.

'Alan! So it really is you.'

I took his outstretched hand.

'Hullo, Peter. What brings you here?'

He sat down, carefully hitching up his trousers.

'I work here. Business administrator. Was up in town yesterday; only got back last night. When I heard you'd been brought in, the name rang a bell. Hope they're taking care of you.' He gestured expansively. 'If they're not, just complain to the management.' He sat back. 'Well, well. It's been quite a time, hasn't it?'

I agreed. I looked at him. He seemed much more assured in his manner than when we had been students at Glasgow University and shared digs one winter. He had been reading Arts; my principal subject was physics.

'When did you come down here?' I asked.

'Oh, about three years ago. I took a business diploma at Strathclyde and came here. What about you?'

'I did my Ph.D. work in Edinburgh then spent some years with NASA at Goddard. In fact I only came back to Glasgow last summer.'

He grinned. 'Brain drain in reverse. And you're connected with this tracking station at Low Glenadale?'

'Yes. I was on my way to spend a few weeks working there. Which reminds me. When do you think I'll be allowed out of here?'

He shrugged. 'Up to the quacks. Who's looking after you?'

'A Dr Selkirk.'

'Oh, Jane. Has she seen you yet this morning?'

Jane, I thought. But not plain Jane. 'No.'

'Oh well, she'll be round anytime now. I must say you look healthy enough.' He crossed his knees, locked his hands round the upper one. 'Where are you staying?'

'At the Outstation, in the bunkhouse.'

'Sounds desperately primitive.'

'Not really. Lets you be on the spot when things are doing.'

'I see.' He tilted his head to one side. 'Married yet?'

'No.'

'Nor am I. But I've met the most marvellous girl,' he went on enthusiastically. This is where I came in, I thought amusedly. 'And this time, Alan, I know she's the one. You must meet her. In fact, this is Thursday. Why not spend the weekend at Borgadel House with us?'

He was going too fast for me. Borgadel House—a hotel? Boarding house? Or is it his house? Meanwhile Peter prattled on.

'You'll be able to meet mother again, Alan.'

'That'll be nice,' I lied.

'And Gran. You've never met her. She's a wonderful old soul.'

Gran. Quite suddenly the pieces of jigsaw he'd showered on me began to come together. Old Mrs Campbell, Borgadel House, the David Campbell Neurological Institute, Peter Campbell, business administrator. I began to recall family details Peter had given me when we were students.

'Of course we'll have to wait until they let you go.' He rose to his feet. 'I'll look in again after the doctor's been round.' He grinned. 'Good to see you again, Alan.'

Alone again, I thought about Peter as I'd known him. The father, a likable, talented neurosurgeon, had been in practice in Glasgow; the mother, cool, brittle and bigoted, a keen committee and charity worker, had ruled her husband's and son's lives like a one-woman thought police force. Campbell senior had conformed—it was easy enough for him to do so when most of his attention lay in his work; Peter, in the usual confusion of young manhood, had alternated between an obedience which was a conditioned reflex of childhood and rational rebellion. In particular, Peter had had many girl friends discouraged by his mother's tactics '. . . Jean is so unsuitable and you've your career to think about . . .', apart from illuminating little remarks to the girls that made them step back in dismayed horror at the thought of such a mother-in-law.

Before I knew Peter and his mother well, I'd been shocked that any modern young man could allow himself to be ground into submission so easily; later I observed with awed fascination the implacable manner in which she beat down all opposition on Peter's part, arguing, advancing and publishing her views with a tireless tenacity that shredded away all opposition like the teeth of piranha stripping flesh from the bones of a victim. Equally fascinating was her complete certainty in being right. Her model of the universe was the definitive one and all others were brand X. Beware imitations. Doubtless, too, when she got to heaven, she would put God straight on a few matters.

Peter staged one successful revolt when he managed—I don't remember how—to get his father to take rooms for him near the University during his final year. He shared them with me. We became firm friends and it was then that I came to learn the incubus Peter's mother played in his life. Inevitably, however, our very different careers after graduation separated us. We exchanged two or three letters; I went to his father's funeral the winter after graduation but apart from seeing Peter then, we had no more meetings—until this morning.

Well, I thought, the hospital room breaking in again, there's no sign of a gap in these memories. Before I had time to try to recall what Peter had told me about his grandmother, Nurse Macdonald ushered in Dr Selkirk.

With quiet, friendly efficiency she put me through a number of tests to gauge the extent of my progress, while Nurse Macdonald stood by all starched and crisp with dignity. I found the process not unpleasant, especially when she leant forward and looked at the pupils of my eyes—a good guide to the degree of concussion, she said. I noted again the deep hazel shade of her own eyes and how nicely shaped her mouth was, the lips slightly parted as she examined my—I supposed—bloodshot eyes. I was conscious of the faint caress of her breath on my face and inwardly scolded myself for wondering what would happen if I leaned forward and kissed her. She drew back and I wondered if my eyes had given me away for I thought I detected a tiny glint of amusement in hers. Ah! imagination, the thespian buffoon inside me sighed.

'Not bad,' she said. 'Now I'd like you to get out of bed. Just to test your balance.'

When I stood up and my bare feet touched the cold floor I gasped as a hot flash of pain exploded in my left ankle. I collapsed on the edge of the bed. There followed an examination, the arrival of a wheel-chair, a self-conscious trip along tiled corridors to the X-ray theatre, some modified gymnastics while invisible beams of electrons struck radiation from tungsten targets to explore my foot. Once back in my bed, I lay and waited, wondering gloomily if a plaster cast would be the next item on the agenda.

My forebodings were unfulfilled. When Dr Selkirk returned she smiled cheerfully.

'Just a sprain; we'll strap it up. A few days spent with the minimum of weight on it and it'll be back to normal.'

'When can I leave?'

'I'd like you to spend another night here, just to be on the safe side, especially now we find you have that sprain.' Her lips twitched. 'It'll keep you off your foot and in any case it'll help your concussion. It's a deceptive business. You probably feel all right but you'd really be best to avoid work for a few days, keep out of bright light and generally laze about. I wouldn't do much reading either, if I were you.' She stopped at the door. 'If you behave yourself we'll let you go tomorrow.'

A taciturn sister, whose name I never learned, arrived shortly afterwards to bandage my ankle, assisted docilely and demurely by Macdonald. Alone again, I lay back and inspected my small world once more, the white bed-cover, the chair, the lime-green blinds, the slow secular change in the patterns of sunlight, the pale cream doors of the wardrobe. I remembered the earphones hanging above my head. The jungle rhythms of the latest monosyllabic number one hit in the top ten were percolating through my uncritical brain when the door opened and Peter returned. I removed the earphones.

'I had a word with Dr Selkirk. She told me about your ankle. I mentioned the possibility of you spending the weekend at Borgadel House and she thought it an excellent idea. What do you feel about it?' His round face looked anxiously at me as if the outbreak of nuclear war depended upon my answer. Ah well, I thought, if I'm not allowed to work for a few days. . . . In any case, it'd be good to natter over old times with Peter and—my curiosity prodded me—to see how he'd matured.

I grinned and held out my wrists, handcuff fashion.

'I don't seem to have much choice. Tell Dr Selkirk that I agree to be released into your custody tomorrow.'

'Fine! Fine!' He bounced to the door. There he looked back. 'Incidentally, are you still interested in psychical research and all that stuff?'

'Yes.'

He grinned sharply—with relief?—said 'Fine!' again and shot out before I could say anything. I thought for a bit about the relief that I'd detected then dismissed it since I could have imagined it. When Nurse Macdonald came in half an hour later I managed to persuade her to bring me a newspaper after promising to spend no more than a few minutes reading it. I glanced through the sheets. The continuing story of mankind unfolded itself with its usual mixture of ability and idiocy. I read for only ten minutes before I found my head beginning to ache—serves you right for disobeying doctor's orders, the Calvinistic part of me commented masochistically—and threw the paper to the foot of the bed. A minute later Nurse Macdonald announced another visitor. This time it was Dr Black from the Outstation. He assured himself that I was progressing satisfactorily and told me that the professor had sent von Neumann down to assist him. We talked shop for some time before he left after making me promise to ring up if I required anything.

After lunch Macdonald insisted brightly that 'we should be all the better if we had a little sleep'. In fact 'we' were not too unwilling since 'our' head was pounding dully. The tablets she gave me helped and I slept for a few hours, wakening without a headache just before supper.

I felt an irrational mood of disappointment when a white-coated middle-aged doctor turned up for the evening round instead of Dr Selkirk. He introduced himself as Dr Preston, chatted for a minute or two in pleasant, if slightly aloof, fashion then left. Even doctors must have some off-time, I supposed. Nurse Macdonald was also off-duty. I spent the evening trudging over a desert of boredom and by ten I was glad to capitulate and lie down.

In the quietness I watched the moonlight paint the inside of the room door and tried to sidle round the memory block in an attempt to recover the lost hour. It was no good. I still got as far as Ballochroy but no farther. But again, just as my consciousness dissolved, the screen of my defences down, the twisted, terrified face that had floated before me the previous night presented itself in mute, agonised appeal, so that I jerked awake, my forehead wet, my heart pounding. It was some time before I could edge myself gingerly back into sleep.

2 Knox had a name for them

I left the David Campbell Neurological Institute about 10 a.m. the following morning. Someone had found a strong thick stick to help me hirple along the polished corridor to the main door. Peter carried my belongings in two holdalls, salvaged from the car; Nurse Macdonald hovered anxiously beside me like a small trim tug around an ocean liner. I had grown quite fond of Macdonald. Dr Selkirk had looked in an hour previously and had pronounced me seaworthy in a strictly limited way. When shaking hands, she had warned me to take things easy and to return if I didn't seem to be making progress, I thanked her and found myself wondering in the way one does if I would ever see her again.

I edged crabwise down the front steps. The Friday morning sunshine was dazzling in its brilliance and once in the front passenger seat of Peter's Lincoln-green Vauxhall Viva I lost no time in screening my eyes with the sunglasses from the top pocket of my worn sports jacket. While Peter slung my luggage into the back seat and took his place beside me, I looked round with interest. The Institute, obviously modern, was a flat-roofed, two-storeyed building set in extensive grass-covered grounds dotted with clumps of pine trees and rhododendron bushes.

The car moved forward, its tyres hissing over the brick-red gravel and I began to have misgivings.

'Look, Peter, are you certain this is a good idea? It's extremely kind of you and at any other time I'd love to accept your hospitality but in this lame duck condition am I not going to be a problem to you and your people at Borgadel House?'

'Nonsense. It'll do you good. All you need do is loaf around and turn up for meals. The house is so big you won't get in anyone's way. And I know mother will be pleased to see you again'—ha, ha, I thought—'and I'm sure you and Gran will get on famously.' He darted a glance across at me. Again that trace of anxiety, I wondered, then his gaze was fixed on the winding road once more. 'And Alison. I think you'll like her.' His last remark was carefully casual.

I made my injured foot more comfortable and thought: the man who came to dinner. Which reminded me.

'I was going to be roughing it at the Outstation and so I don't have any presentable clothes in these bags.'

'No excuses. We don't dress for dinner or anything like that.'

Which was a good thing for I certainly hadn't brought my penguin outfit. I shrugged and decided to practise Confucius' advice to the young lady—if you can't avoid it relax and enjoy it.

We had turned on to the road through Low Cattadale. To the south-west the land fell away to Carskiey Bay. The morning air was so clear that the coast of Ireland could be seen painted in a light blue wash along the horizon. At South Carrine Peter took the right fork and crossed Lephenstrath Bridge over the Breackerie Water. A mile on, the Strone Glen cut back through the hills to our right, with the shimmering cobalt-blue sea half a mile to our left. The road now slid round the brown flank of the hills above the small, almost circular valley in which the fishing village of Port Mean lies. We passed the junction where the road branches, the left hand fork diving steeply to the Port houses. Two hundred yards further on, closed, ornamental, wrought-iron lodge gates appeared to the left. A white-painted notice board with the legend *'Private Grounds. No Trespassers'* stood sentrywise at the entrance.

Peter grinned, stopped the car and got out to open the gates. I sat still, cloaked with uselessness as with a garment.

We drove along a winding road between an abundant growth of bushes, mostly of the ubiquitous rhododendron family, many of them thirty feet in height. Ultimately we emerged from the shrubs and I got my first view of Borgadel House. It was one of those massive sandstone Victorian mansions you find so many of still scattered in surprisingly lonely places on the west coast of Scotland. It probably contained twenty rooms, some of which could easily have enclosed a modern prefab cottage. Standing on a broad balustraded terrace, its tall windows and imposing portico reminded me of the illustrations in *Country Life*.

A uniformed maid opened the door. Once in the spacious hall, Peter handed over my holdalls.

'The bedrooms are mostly upstairs, Alan, but there is one downstairs that we've given you.'

I thanked him. We proceeded, as the police put it, across the hall, turned left along a corridor and stopped outside the second door on the left. Peter opened it for the maid and ushered me into a large comfortably furnished bedroom. I limped across to the brightly-curtained window and looked out across the sunlit drive and park. A broad belt of fir trees bordered the rolling green slopes. I was more than ever reminded of something out of *Country Life*. The only incongruous note was the top of a TV mast appearing beyond the trees.

'A bit different from the digs in Kersland Street,' I remarked.

He grinned in response. 'Something better than your bunkhouse, anyway.' He went to the door. 'I'll come back in ten minutes, Alan. We'll have coffee. And then I'm afraid I'll have to return to the Institute. By the way, the bathroom is next door.' He and the maid left and I sank back on the edge of the bed, my leg stretched out, until the pain in my ankle had subsided by a few dols. I unpacked my belongings and placed the small bottle of tablets they'd given me on the bedside table beside the lamp. Alan the addict, I thought. I caught myself trying to force apart the shutters over my memory and shook my head in vexation at my failure. The dull blank in my mind was still unnerving. Again I felt that sense of urgency, of insecurity and near panic somehow associated with the lost episode. That policeman: had he been telling the truth? I felt suffocated, almost sick.

Sitting there on the edge of the bed I felt swept up in a vortex. And then, I suddenly saw the steady hazel eyes of Jane Selkirk and I calmed down. I wiped my forehead, shook a tablet from the bottle, limped to the wash-hand basin on the right and washed the pill down. The cold water helped. In the mirror I saw my taut reflection anxiously regarding me above the beaded tumbler: same old features, same slightly bent nose, same half-inch scar that bisected my right eyebrow, relic of a rugby game. Against my dark hair above my left ear, a white Elastoplast dressing covered the cut on my head.

There was a knock on the door. When Peter came in, he glanced at me.

'You look a bit peaky. Are you all right?'

'Yes, bloody but unbowed.' I forced a smile. In truth the nasty moment was largely over, hastened on its way by my recollection that Dr Selkirk had told me that concussion often had occasional delayed after effects. I hoped they didn't occur too often.

In the hall, Peter steered me to a door on the opposite side. We entered a vast sitting-room in which, in spite of the season, a coal fire burned in the large stone hearth flanked by black, iron dogs. The room was not too warm, however. Under wide oriel diamond-paned windows, a chintz-covered window seat curved. A desk carrying a portable typewriter and other secretarial effects caught sunlight within the window bay. Two couches and several armchairs were grouped round the fire. To my left a magnificent Bechstein grand with music on it occupied most of a large alcove. The walls carried oil-paintings, mostly sea- or land-scapes.

A young woman in a blue frock, attractive in a quiet, gentle way, with fair hair caught back almost to the nape of her neck, was busy at a trolley laden with coffee things. She had her back to us when we entered but straightened up and turned. Her smile, obviously directed at Peter, transformed her face. Seated on the couch to the left of the fireplace was an elderly woman in her seventies, with a plump, rosy face and spunsilk white hair. She was comfortably stout with a placid expression on her face. She wore a fawn woollen dress.

'Gran, this is Alan; Alan, this is Alison Cadell.'

When she spoke, Mrs Campbell's voice was light, but with a faint asthmatic overtone.

'I'm glad to meet you, Alan—I shall call you Alan if I may'—I nodded—'and I hope you'll soon be back to normal. Please feel quite at home—we have a very informal life here. If you want to rest, please do so. I know you must take things easy. I suspect Peter has really asked you here to back him up against a house full of women.' She gave her grandson a look of affection—it was obvious they were very fond of each other. 'Now please be seated and Alison will pour coffee.'

I sat down facing the fire, my stick on the carpet beside my chair. I began to relax as conversation developed. Alison Cadell appeared to be Mrs Campbell's secretary. I thought Peter's grandmother was quite conscious of the feelings her grandson and secretary had towards each other. Finally Peter stood up, after refusing a second cup.

'Sorry to dash away like this but I have to get back. I'll see you before dinner, Alan. If you're wanting something to read, the library is across the hall. It's a bit of a hotchpotch but you might find something.'

A quarter of an hour later, Alison herself left to go into Campbeltown and I chatted for half an hour or so with Mrs Campbell.

I gained the impression of a kindly, intelligent personality. There was something of Queen Victoria in her later years about her, though much mellower and more approachable (and certainly more easily amused!). She had in fact been born in Port Mean. Her husband came from Campbeltown. By a combination of good fortune and innate native brilliance he had become so wealthy in shipping that they could afford to buy Borgadel House just prior to the Second World War. It was during that war that Colin was killed. The father died some years later.

He had managed to outmanœuvre the Inland Revenue

over death duties so that the estate, still growing rapidly, passed virtually intact to Mrs Campbell. When her second son died so unexpectedly she had established the David Campbell Neurological Institute and encouraged and held a small team of researchers by giving them their head and a rich Foundation to tap. And finally, her daughter-in-law and grandson had come to live with her, the grandson finding a useful position in the Institute and in helping to run the estate. Some of this I learned from Mrs Campbell; Peter filled me in on the other details later.

'I shall leave you now,' the old lady said. 'No, please don't get up. I have to rest, too, but in my case it's age and not accident.' She moved quite spryly to the door. 'I had 'flu not so long ago and although I feel perfectly fit, the doctor, tiresome fellow, insists I have a rest before lunch. I'll see you then.'

I was looking at a *Glasgow Herald* in the warm, quiet room when I became conscious someone had entered. Again I was told solicitously not to rise—almost as if I wore a label saying 'Fragile—breaks easily'. The newcomer was a woman, in her late thirties, I supposed, wearing a claret jumper and grey skirt. She had thick black hair swept back from her brow on to the crown of her head; her face was unobtrusively made-up to make the most of dark, arching eyebrows and slightly gamin features.

'You're Dr Ramsay, I'm Dorothy West, Mrs Campbell's housekeeper. Are you quite comfortable?'

I assured her I was and we exchanged a few weather and geographical comments while she tossed some logs of wood on to the hissing fire. Suddenly I remembered where I had seen her before—at Peter's father's funeral. But she had been their housekeeper then, a sort of housekeeper-secretary—with Peter's mother so devoted to committees and good works, they had needed one. I reminded her of our former meeting.

'Yes, that's right. When Dr Campbell died and old Mrs Campbell invited Peter and his mother to make their home here, I was asked to come too. It was fortunate she required a secretary at the time.'

'Don't you find it a bit quiet here after town?'

She sat down in an armchair opposite me—I was on a couch at one side of the crackling fire—and smoothed down her skirt.

'It is quiet but it has advantages. And we do have a certain amount of social life. In any case I have plenty of time off and it's quite easy to reach Glasgow from here.'

I wondered about her background. She was obviously well-educated and bright. Almost as if in reply to my thought she added: 'Anyway I got enough of kicking around the world when I was in the Wrens. I left them to be with my mother before she died then took the position with Peter's family almost as a stopgap.' She shrugged. 'In fact I spent five years with them—and now I've been five years down here as well.' Just for a moment she looked almost sulky as if she wasn't all that contented with her lot and I recalled with interest what Peter had told me one evening in digs when he was complaining of his mother's blighting attitude to any friendships with the opposite sex.

'In fact, Alan,' he said bitterly, 'I might have gone queer the way she pushed me off women if it hadn't been for our housekeeper. When I was on vacation in my first year at university, she, well, balanced the books, so to speak.'

Throughout that summer, whenever the absence of the parents allowed, she had conducted with enthusiastic efficiency an extramural class for one in a subject that, for all our permissive society, is not yet taught in such a practical way. A spark of pure enjoyment glowed within me when I pictured Peter's mother's face if she had known she had nurtured this viper in her bosom (she was much given to such phrases). The viper, in fact still very attractive, rose.

'Have you seen the library?'

'No, but I'd like to.'

She led me across the wide hall to a door opposite. Having opened it, she excused herself and left me to explore beyond.

The library was large, almost as spacious as the sitting-room. Facing me was a veined marble fireplace on either side of which was a closed, cream-coloured door. Also before me and in the middle of the room was a massive oval polished table with one central pillar supporting it. Seven chairs stood around it. A large french window set in the left-hand wall admitted sunlight.

I leaned on my stick and studied the titles of the volumes. It was, as Peter had remarked, a veritable hotchpotch. Books on the history of Scotland; volumes on shipping; novels, Scott and Dickens being well represented; hard-cover Edgar Wallace and other crime authors of that vintage; gardening books, medical books; volumes on spiritualism and religion including the two volume edition of Myers' *Human Personality and its Survival of Bodily Death* and Elliot Rose's *A Razor for a Goat; Problems in the History of Witchcraft and Diabolism*; paperbacks, an out-of-date edition of the *Encyclopaedia Britannica*—you could have conducted a kind of literary archaeological research here, classifying and dating the successive cultures that had contributed their remains to the collection. It was, however, the sort of library I like and I was still browsing when someone began to beat a small gong. It took me seven minutes to make a quick wash and brush-up before hobbling along to the dining-room.

When I entered the room, old Mrs Campbell was at the head of the table being helped into her place by Alison Cadell. Dorothy West was there, too. And there were two other women present. One was Peter's mother, outwardly unchanged, still slim, taut, elegant. She was talking to a plumpish, rather flamboyantly dressed woman of a reluctant fifty with a round, powdered, slightly knowing, face topped by a beehive hairstyle of improbable black. She was introduced to me as Mrs Davenport. Peter's mother also shook hands, commiserated with me about my accident and assured me how pleased she was to see me after such a long time. I returned the lie and cursed both Peter and myself under my breath, him for suggesting I came here, me for accepting. Knox had a phrase, I thought, something about a monstrous regiment of women.

During the meal most of the conversation was made by the two Mrs Campbells, Mrs Davenport and myself. They professed an interest in my work, of course (encourage a man to relax by asking him about himself or his work); I did my best to explain geodesy and radio astronomy to them. Mrs Davenport listened with a distinct air of being apart from it all, interjecting a few cryptic remarks to the effect that such studies were all very well but inadequate in understanding the universe. She had an 'if I would, what a tale I could unfold' aura about her that for some reason inspired a strange sense of familiarity, although I was sure I had never seen her before. At least . . . I found myself pause, the dull ache in my head reminding me of my recent loss of memory and insinuating a soft 'how can you be sure?' I discovered I was staring blindly at Alison Cadell and looked away.

It appeared that Mrs Davenport had arrived by plane at Machrihanish Airport that morning and would be staying until Monday. She had had a pleasant flight, she assured us, 'and we must hope that our meetings will be crowned with success'. At this point Dorothy West looked cynical and met my eye; I merely looked blank. Alison Cadell seemed impressed while the old lady appeared almost anxious. I transferred my attention to Peter's mother and found her gazing with implacable dislike at Alison. She caught my gaze and a bland mask slid over her face like a welder's helmet. That at least was familiar ground and I began to speculate during the dessert of lemon meringue pie whether Peter would at last be mature enough to marry Alison in spite of his mother.

Mrs Campbell senior was asking how Mrs Davenport wished to spend the afternoon. Mrs Davenport took a sip of coffee while she considered the question.

'I shall rest part of the afternoon,' she said briskly, 'and then I shall walk quietly in the grounds. I find it helps.'

Why did she seem so familiar? I looked at her with renewed interest as a possibility suggested itself to me and it began to make some sort of sense.

'And what about you, Alan?'

'I think it'd be best if I just staggered around or rested, just as I find it suits me,' I said apologetically. Old antisocial Alan.

In fact, after coffee, I collected the first volume of

Myers' *Human Personality* from the library and returned to my room. But the sunshine drew me out of the house. Putting on my sunglasses, I limped across the flagstoned terrace and descended the broad, shallow, uneven steps to the lawn. I crossed the close-cut grass, trying to convince myself my ankle had improved, the sun's rays warm on head and shoulders. After sixty yards of the gently-sloping lawn I came to the closely-packed bushes and fir trees forming the border. A gravel path curled off through the undergrowth and I followed it, coming before long to a second open area with a seat beside a weathered and cone-topped small wooden building perched on the seaward edge of this area. The building was a summerhouse, octagonal in shape with dark brown branches nailed in lozenge patterns across the once white walls, now peeling and shabby. There was a door in the side facing me; no windows were visible until I walked up to the building and saw that the windows were in the four seaward sides. Below them the ground fell away almost sheerly to a cinnamon beach hundreds of feet below.

I turned the verdigrised door-handle and pushed. It was so stiff that at first I thought it was locked but in fact age and many winters' weathering had simply warped the door and rusted the hinges. It scraped open, a part of me cursing myself because the effort had jarred my ankle. Once inside, the door closed behind me without much force being required.

The interior was quite unusual. There was a central, circular, green-painted table bolted to the floor and a wooden bench running round the walls. But what caught my attention was the way in which every square inch of the inside walls and ceiling had been lined with fir-cones, their points facing outwards. There must have been tens of thousands of them, brown and dry, carefully marshalled by size to produce rather pleasing patterns. Right in the centre of the ceiling there was the grand-daddy of all fir-cones; circling him were ones of lesser size until those satellites at the ceiling edge barely measured a centimetre across. It was a bit like being inside a beehive.

I crossed to the window and sat down. The window was

dusty on the inside but not at all opaque and the greenhouse effect made the interior warm. I leaned back, the cone-tips knuckling my back through my shirt, and wondered who the summerhouse builder had been—local carpenter? gardener? member of the family?

My thoughts, by no means high-powered, had meandered into a flatland of reverie and I was thinking I had better move on before I dozed off completely when I suddenly heard voices, soft, low-pitched. They came from outside the summerhouse. I sat still while I considered what to do. Cough loudly, burst into song or remain quiet. Even without any desire to hear I began to make sense of the words though the whispers were so quiet that they held no clue to the age or sex of the speakers.

'. . . and you'll be careful?'

'Yes. You're sure there's no danger?'

'None. We'll take care of him at the other place until he's ready.'

'And I'll keep an eye on the other. Just in case.'

'Yes, do that.'

I found my mouth dry. The voices were dying away even while I froze there, staring at the fir-coned walls. All sorts of startled speculations scurried through my mind as I overcame inertia and limped to the door. It stuck; half a dozen tugs and finally I swung it back. Descending the two brown sandstone steps I scanned the open, green area, bright in the sunlight. There was no one to be seen. I stepped forward, was reminded by the stabs of pain in my ankle that I had forgotten my stick and halted. I re-ran what I had heard of the whispered conversation and wondered why I had been so disturbed. The sentences were capable of a number of innocent explanations—perhaps the words 'careful' and 'danger' spoken in such low, secretive tones had alerted me to the possibility of an unpleasant interpretation. I stood there, uneasy, then turned back into the summerhouse to retrieve my stick.

I mooched slowly along the steep edge of the enclosure. As well as the entrance to the path I had used, there was a second gap in the semi-circle of trees and shrubs. It lay near the cliff-edge and marked the top of a narrow path that swooped unevenly down the side of the scarp to the beach far below. I wondered if the speakers had come up that way.

For the remainder of the afternoon I rested on the bed in my room, the curtains drawn. In fact I fell asleep and woke about six in that dull, dry-mouthed daze you often experience if you have an afternoon nap. After a cold shower I felt better.

In the sitting-room I found Peter and his mother. Margaret Campbell stood looking out of the oriel window; Peter sat sulkily on the sofa to the left of the fire. As I entered he said irritably:

'But I agree with you, Mother. I don't like it either—or her, for that matter. But what can one do?'

His mother swung round, saw me and switched what she was about to say.

'Have you told Alan yet?'

'No, not yet. There's time enough during the weekend and anyway he's not up to par yet.'

I stood like a dummy just inside the door wondering what the hell was going on. Mrs Campbell came forward, smiling: somehow she always reminded me of Lady Macbeth.

'Alan! Come in. How are you feeling now?'

'Not so bad.' My eyes flicked from mother to son. 'What's up?'

Peter shrugged. 'It's nothing'—his mother moved impatiently—'well, that's not quite right but I'm not sure you can help. Oh blast! Sit down, Alan.' I lowered myself carefully into the armchair facing the fire. 'When I invited you for the weekend I'm afraid I had a slight ulterior motive.' He hesitated. 'It's Gran.' My mind blanked. 'I take it you met Mrs Davenport at lunch?'

'Yes.'

'Well, she was introduced or recommended to Gran by old Mrs Aitkenhead, a friend of Gran's. She's a medium.'

So I'd been right.

'I can't say I've heard of her—is she any good?'

Mother and son spoke together, Peter a shade before his mother.

'That's not the point . . .'

'What do you mean?—is she any good? It's all nonsense! She's simply out to batten on to Mother's obsession. It's—it's criminal! Frauds and charlatans the lot of them. They should be locked up.'

So much for a century of psychical research—possibly the most complicated research subject in existence. I didn't even feel irritated by Mrs Campbell's attitude; previous experience had cured me of the expectation that most people could approach the subject rationally. A phrase from Claire Stewart's recent book *Through A Glass Darkly* surfaced in my memory: 'For the majority of mankind, the enchanted mirror of psychical research merely reflects the doppelgangers of their own fears and prejudices.'

'They're not all frauds,' I said mildly. 'I doubt if more than a tenth are.' Though I privately reserved judgement on Mrs Davenport.

Margaret Campbell's eyes blazed.

'That's not the point. It's not good for Mother to be excited like this. And it's morbid.'

Oh sure, I thought, and they all go mad in the end.

Peter leaned forward. 'We *are* worried, Alan. She's not too well—her heart isn't too strong. But apart from that we don't want her to get too deeply involved in this thing and then, when she gets disillusioned, suffer too much of a letdown.'

When, not if.

'But spiritualism brings comfort to millions of people.' I was being deliberately obtuse for I wasn't sure I liked the idea of my old buddy-buddy Peter and his mother trying to interfere with the old lady's wishes, even if they were acting from the best intentions. I thought that losing a husband and two sons entitled her to a little comfort. Her daughter-in-law's lips thinned.

'A Christian has no need of such mumbo-jumbo.'

Peter's head moved wearily. 'Yes, Mother.' He turned to me again. 'Ordinary spiritualism, yes. If she became a member of a spiritualist church I don't think I'd mind . . .'

'I would!' his mother interjected.

'. . . but this is different.'

'In what way?'

'I've heard that this woman specialises in physical phenomena.'

My eyes narrowed. That was an entirely different kettle of fish. Physical phenomena, from simple table-rappings to full-blown materialisations, had been thick on the ground during the end of the nineteenth and the first third of the twentieth centuries but since the Second World War had become almost as scarce as Liberal governments. Some unkind people held that the invention of the infra-red image converter, enabling investigators to see the seance room in pitch darkness, was positively correlated with the decline of the physical side of mediumship. Certainly since some members of the Society for Psychical Research offered a reward of £250 for a physical phenomenon that could be observed through the infra-red snooperscope, there had been a conspicuous absence of physical mediums volunteering for such serious investigation. At the same time, however, I knew that in various places in Britain, mostly in the dimly-lit sitting-rooms of private houses, seances still took place at which the sitters, usually fervent believers, saw white misty shapes, heard sounds and felt tables rock 'when the conditions were right'. Whether the conditions referred to opportunities for fraud or related to the barrier between this world and the next was a moot point. The important point was that physical phenomena exercised a peculiar fascination for many who yearned to contact dead loved ones and hooked them as surely as heroin creates drug addicts.

'I see what you mean, Peter,' I said slowly. The door-knob clicked behind me and I saw Peter and his mother assume wooden, neutral expressions. I turned my head.

'Good evening,' said Mrs Davenport, flashing her white smile as if she personally had invented the celebrated ring of confidence. 'I've had a most enjoyable afternoon. The grounds are absolutely delightful. I feel most refreshed.'

3 The museum of childhood

At dinner we had the same complement as at lunch, with the addition of Peter. Conversation remained general, ranging easily from weather through holidays, travel allowances, customs, politics and the theatre until coffee was served. Alison mentioned how impressed she'd been as a child when she'd seen a performance of Barrie's *Mary Rose*. I seized the opportunity to guide the conversation a little.

'Yes, I saw it once as a student. A rep company did it at the King's. The funny thing is that although at the time I thought it terribly twee I had second thoughts the following summer when I was hiking up in the north-west of Scotland beyond the Great Glen. It must be the loneliest area in the British Isles. You can walk for mile upon mile and not see a human habitation.'

'And yet, Alan,' old Mrs Campbell put in gently, 'there was a time, before the Clearances, when tens of thousands of people farmed there.'

I nodded. 'I wonder if that explains what I felt. I had been walking all morning across the moors when I came to this glen. The sun was very hot and when I was halfway up the glen I stopped to rest and have a meal. There were hills all around. There was a little stream—I could hear it splash over some rocks—the only other sounds were the buzzing of bees and the occasional cry of a bird.' I glanced round the table as I concocted my anecdote; the audience was gratifyingly attentive. 'I had only begun to eat when I had the overwhelming sensation of being watched, not by one but by many. I looked round but of course the glen was empty. I tried to concentrate on my food but the impression grew in intensity; a new element entered, resentment thick and heavy as a blanket.' I laughed shortly. 'Silly of me but it affected me so much that I packed up, left the glen and went round by another road. Years later I learned that the factor who cleared that glen in 1782 in rather brutal fashion was an Alan Ramsay.'

There were suitable murmurs from my listeners though I thought I detected a healthy spark of scepticism in Dorothy West's eye. I pressed on.

'It's the only experience of that kind I've ever had. A poor one, but mine own.'

Mrs Davenport put down her coffee-cup. 'But how interesting. You must be sensitive.'

'Sensitive?'

'Yes, you must have the talent. Undeveloped, of course.'

I simulated slight alarm and honest doubt. 'Do you mean I have, what's it called, psychic powers?' Peter's mother's face registered annoyed confusion; her son was schooling his features to a studied blankness. Mrs Davenport bent slightly towards me, rather as a Royal Academician might expand towards a young painter whose work showed untutored promise.

'It's possibly very slight, you know, and it may well have been *ruined* beyond recall by your scientific conditioning but when you had that experience you *did* have the talent.'

'Oh come now. I'm not even the seventh son of a seventh son. And anyway I probably just had a touch of liver or something that day.'

The Davenport beehive hairstyle shook chidingly.

'I think I detect rationalisation! So many are scared of these things, of the world of spirit, that they shut the doors of their minds to any manifestations.'

'Oh, I try to keep an open mind. I've read quite a bit about Rhine's work on telepathy and I admit he makes quite a case for it.' If Mrs Davenport was sincere it must have been painful for her—as painful as it is for the artist meeting the clot who thinks modern art is all nonsense but 'knows what he likes'. As if on cue, Peter came in.

'Perhaps I should tell you, Alan, before you really put your foot in it, that Mrs Davenport is a medium herself.'

'Oh really.' I essayed confusion and interest. 'I hope I haven't said anything that annoyed you.'

'Not at all.' Pardon graciously granted. Old Mrs Campbell's slightly breathy voice intervened.

'Mrs Davenport has kindly come down this weekend to give me a number of sittings, Alan.'

'Oh.' I hoped I was still giving the right impression of the atheist at a church wedding.

Mrs Davenport took pity on me.

'Mrs Campbell, perhaps Dr Ramsay could, if he cares, form one of our circle of sitters tomorrow evening after dinner. Not tonight, of course, in our preliminary sitting or tomorrow afternoon which is again private to you and me, but at nine tomorrow night.' The late, late show for me. 'He may well turn out to be a strong sitter with his talent.'

Peter's grandmother's kindly expression aroused a qualm of conscience.

'Do you feel like joining us, Alan? You needn't, of course, if you don't feel up to it.'

'I'd be delighted to, thank you.'

Peter grinned. 'I'll be there and Alison. And I think Dorothy said she'd be present. Oh, and one or two from the Institute.'

I knew by the tight expression on his mother's face that she had no intention of joining the happy circle.

'I hope,' said Mrs Davenport, 'that conditions will be favourable.'

So did I. I also hoped as we rose from the table that Peter and his mum appreciated the fact that I was in the position of a plumber who had forgotten his tools—no infra-red source and telescope, no camera or tape recorder, no thermometers, magnetometers or photo-electric cells, no nothing.

Mrs Davenport retired with Peter's grandmother, Dorothy West excused herself and Peter, his mother, Alison and I returned to the sitting-room. Margaret Campbell challenged me. 'Well, Alan, you've succeeded in getting in to attend this preposterous nonsense tomorrow night. Do you think you'll catch that odious woman at her tricks? It's the only way we'll convince Mother she's a fraud.'

I sighed. It would be downright impossible to convince her of the difficulty of supervising adequately the seance room phenomena when control wasn't in my hands. I sought for words, the search made harder because of the return of the dull bruised ache to my head.

'I'll do my best, Mrs Campbell. I'll discuss it with Peter. We'll do all we can.'

'I hope so.' She bit her lip. 'It's a pity it wasn't tonight then she wouldn't get the opportunity to influence Mother.' Her face became bleak. 'Oh, it's damnable.' And indeed it must have been infinitely frustrating for her when she once had been absolute ruler in her own home. She breathed deeply, looked at us each in turn, then relaxed. Her mouth acted out a smile.

'Well, I'll leave you young people to yourselves.'

After she'd left us, Peter went over to the drinks table.

'What'll you have, Alan?'

'I'd better not.'

He looked at me.

'Mother's really steamed up about this, isn't she?' He grinned. 'Almost like old times.'

Alison took a gin and tonic from him. I thought she looked almost frail beside him.

'I can sympathise with her, Peter. I dislike that woman intensely.'

'Woman's intuition, darling?' He mixed himself a whisky and soda. She smiled.

'Perhaps. But there's something so smug and sleek about her.' She hesitated. 'And . . .'

'And what?'

She licked her lips. 'I don't know. But I'm worried.'

The throb in my head was worse.

'Where's the seance to be held tomorrow?'

'The library.' Peter looked at me over his glass. 'What have you in mind?'

'Very little, I'm afraid. I'll have another look at the library tomorrow.' After I've had a good night's sleep. 'Do you have a tape recorder?'

'Yes. You want to tape the seance?'

'Yes.' For some time we batted the problem around but finally I had to give up. I got to my feet, apologised for leaving them so early.

'No, no, that's all right, old boy. We tend to forget you only came out of hospital this morning. Anyway, you've got to feel fresh for tomorrow night.'

I nodded, said good night to them and retired to my room. There was still a pale light in the western sky by the time I had completed my preparations for bed and stood at the window, the day's events singing through my head in a jumble of cinema clips without order or editing. The fragment of whispered conversation I had overheard in the summerhouse returned to me and revived my uneasiness. My feeling of inadequacy with respect to Peter's and his mother's expectations of my prowess as a fraud-unveiler also nagged at me. I filled a tumbler with water and washed down one of the long, green, soapy-textured pills then climbed wearily into bed, pulling the cool sheets over me.

It was an hour before I dozed off. My hopes for a refreshing night's sleep seemed groundless, for consciousness returned long before dawn. For a time I lay flat in bed, willing sleep; my head burned dully and the pill I had taken did nothing more for me.

Stretching out my arm, I grabbed my watch and looked at the glowing hands. A quarter past midnight. I pushed the bedclothes aside and padded to the window. Bushes and trees were black shadows splashed over the lawn. I found myself nervously alert. Perhaps a book might do the trick, the more soporific the better. Slipping on trousers over my pyjamas, I picked up my stick and left the room. The corridor was quiet and dark, the only illumination being starlight through its windows. I reached the hall and opened the library door. Closing it behind me, I switched on the lights. The multi-coloured rows of books blazed back at me, making me screw up my eyes in defence. For a few minutes I browsed half-heartedly along the shelves, finally choosing an old fawn, battered account of the history of Kintyre. I was about to leave the room when I noticed that the door on the left of the fireplace was half open. Through the gap, further bookshelves were dimly visible. Curiosity nudged me over to the door. I pushed it half open, stepped through and halted, frozen.

The room was quite small. The light from the library was sufficiently reflected off book shelves to show dimly the smallish curtained window in its black rectangle, what seemed to be glass cases containing an indistinguishable miscellany of objects, a round table and two armchairs, one on either side of a cold, empty fireplace.

The armchairs were occupied.

In the semi-darkness two figures sat in silent, motionless communion, facing each other, as they must have done all the time I was in the other room choosing a book.

For a long moment I stood there, the world a fragile ice sculpture that would shatter at any instant, waiting for either figure to move. They did not stir. Slowly, my heart thumping, I made my left hand search out a light switch. I flicked it down. The sudden flood of light revealed the figures in harsh clarity and I felt my breath rush from my body in the unbelieving shock of recognition that the man facing me was Peter's father—the neurosurgeon whose funeral I had attended five years ago.

Blank-minded, I was still able to note how the figures' absolute stillness matched my own paralysis, though my racing pulse denied the illusion that the clock of time had stopped.

Madame Tussauds! The name screamed from the depths of my mind as realisation of their waxen nature swept over me. I strode forward, the anger of relief burning within me.

The second figure, in the uniform of a major in the British Army, was of a man in his early thirties. He bore a certain facial resemblance to the first who, I now saw, actually had an open book turned face down on the arm of his chair, as if he had been interrupted in his reading. The major, in his turn, held a pipe.

I looked at the waxen simulacra in distaste, the feeling of half-fascination, half-repulsion I had experienced on my one visit to the famous London waxworks conjured up again by their unwarranted mimicry of life, no, of death-in-life. I was turning my attention to the contents of the glass cases when a sound behind me shattered the repair to my calmness. I whirled, pain gouging at my ankle.

The housekeeper stood in the doorway, her head slightly to one side, the merest trace of a smile on her lips. She wore a wine-red ankle-length belted dressing-gown. Her long, dark hair, released from its thick daytime plait, touched her shoulders. Her face, possibly because it was clean of make-up, seemed younger than that of a woman in her late thirties.

'Can't you sleep?' The warm, feminine voice was almost casual in its inquiry.

I took a deep breath. 'No. I came down for a book.' I raised the history of Kintyre, then used it to indicate the dummies. 'Who are they? The door was open so I . . .'

Her dark eyebrows rose and she came closer.

'Dr David Campbell and Major Colin Campbell. The old lady's sons. The room is a sort of museum.' She looked up at me. 'Perhaps shrine would be a better word. The cases are full of every childhood possession the boys had that she still treasured.' And indeed that was true. I now saw that the miscellany under their glass tops included an old red wooden engine, soldiers, a battered cricket bat, a stamp album open at overprinted German stamps, boys' clothes, several school caps, a baby's first shoes in pale blue, a collection of seashells, school notebooks, bundles of letters held together with ribbons, school reports, university scrolls. The collection, appalling in its revelation of maternal pride and grief, went on and on.

I turned and met Mrs West's curious gaze.

'It's unbelievable. She had the figures specially made?'

'Oh yes. She quite often spends hours in here. Usually the door is kept closed. She says that she sees no essential difference between having these reminders of her sons' appearances and having photographs. I can't see it myself.' She shivered, her arms hugging herself below her breasts. 'I think there's something eerie about wax dummies, unhealthy. Yet in all other ways, she is so very sensible.'

She was standing quite close to me. I became conscious of the velvet quietness of the house, of the faint aroma of perfumed soap, the distinct aura of attraction my companion possessed. Our eyes held as the moment lengthened and I was sure I detected growing amusement in hers, plus a knowledge of my awareness of her femininity. I was also aware that if I did anything about it, my head would probably come apart at the seams. She grinned almost mischievously.

'I'm sorry you can't sleep.'

'Oh, it's all right. I think I'll live.'

'Would you like me to bring you some hot chocolate? That often helps.'

'Thank you.'

We switched out the light and left the grotesque little museum. In the hall my companion left me to go to the kitchen while I returned to my room. I brooded unhappily on the implications of the museum's existence until a soft knock on the door prompted me to open it. Dorothy West entered with a glass of drinking chocolate on a saucer. She put it down on the bedside table and straightened up. She smiled.

'That should help you sleep.'

'Thank you.' Nothing, if not polite.

She left the room, glancing back as I began to close the door. I replied to her 'goodnight' and shut it. I found myself smiling as I sat on the bed and sipped the hot drink. In fact, once I'd put out the light and lain down, I slid easily into sleep. If the terrified man walked in the theatre of my subconsciousness, I had no recollection of his visit when the dawn chorus of birds woke me the following morning.

4 A fringe of knowledge . . .

It was while I was consuming eggs and bacon that I realised just how much better I felt. I had no trace of a headache, I felt rested and my ankle was considerably less painful. Mrs Campbell informed me that her mother-in-law always had breakfast in bed. Mrs Davenport assured us that she had a strong presentiment that conditions might well be favourable that evening.

'We had a very interesting and valuable preliminary sitting last night. I was very conscious of a willingness to co-operate from the world of spirit. My control said those dear ones in spirit had been waiting a long time for this opportunity to make contact with those still in the body.'

I watched her audience's varied but familiar reactions. In a materialistic age of TV, radar, bingo, communication satellites and transplant surgery it shocked, disconcerted and almost embarrassed people encountering for the first time someone who seemed to think no more of contacting the spirits of the dead than of popping in for a cuppa with her next-door neighbour. Peter's mother was furious—and scared; Alison seemed baffled but impressed; I thought Peter's sense of humour clashed with his irritation at the glib way our friendly neighbourhood spirit-raiser used the jargon of the trade.

'Something to look forward to,' he said lightly. The laser-beam look his mother shot at him should have drilled a neat cauterised hole through him. For once oblivious to his mother's displeasure, he turned to me.

'What are your plans for today, Alan?'

I shrugged. 'Another lazy day, I suppose. Though I would like to go down to Southend to see how my car is. And,' I said slowly, 'I'd like to see the point where I went off the road.'

'Okay. I'll take you in this morning. I have to go into the Institute in any case. Alison, how about you?'

She shook her head. 'I'd better stay in case your grandmother needs me.'

'Okay. How about having lunch at the Institute, Alan? I could show you around—if you'd be interested.'

We left Borgadel House about nine-fifteen. Sitting beside Peter in the Vauxhall Viva I peered through my sunglasses and thought about the seance. I hoped again that Peter appreciated to some extent how open-ended the whole arrangement was and just how handicapped I was. However, as we descended the hill at Garveld towards the bridge over the Strone Water at Carskiey, I listed for him a few simple requirements he could provide for me. I also briefed him as far as possible on what to watch out for.

'What a nasty suspicious mind you have.'

At South Carrine we turned sharp right and a minute or so later reached the shore at Keil Point. Through Peter's half of the windscreen, across three miles of sun-sparkled sea, Sanda Island was visible, its little brother Sheep Island nestling beside it. Far beyond them the blue and white beehive of Ailsa Craig shimmered silkily in the sunshine.

We ran past the first houses of Southend village. Just before Muneroy's, Peter turned the car right into a narrow lane that ended at Barker's Garage. We left the Viva in the cobbled courtyard and went into the semi-darkness of the garage. Two or three cars and a single-decker bus shared its interior. I spotted the MG 1100 in a corner.

A bulky, grey-haired man of about fifty, wearing grease- and oil-stained dungarees, straightened up from the bonnet of an ancient Ford Popular.

'This is Alan Ramsay,' said Peter. 'His car was brought in on Wednesday. What's the situation?'

'Well now, we took the liberty of going ahead with repairs. We hadn't a spare windscreen but we got one by the carrier from Glasgow and we should have it fitted by late Monday morning at the latest. We've beaten out the dent on the wing and resprayed it. Would you like to look?'

The maroon respray was a perfect match. I was quite content to wait for Monday before using my ankle driving. I thanked him, told him I'd settle up when I collected the car and left. Seeing the MG 1100 again had produced no memory of the crash.

We found the site of the accident easily enough. The tell-tale skid-marks of fused rubber still blackened the tarmacadam and powdered safety glass from the windscreen still littered the road. The grassy bank of the road was scarred deeply by the car wheels.

With the stick point I scuffed a trail through the washing-soda-like glass fragments. Conscious of Peter watching me, I looked around. I had gone into the hedge north of Keprigan between the Brecklate road junction and the point where the burn draining Glen Kerran enters the Conieglen Water. The road was, just as the constable said, quite straight. As I faced south, the hills rose on my right beyond the wire fence; on my left the undergrowth fell away to the Conieglen Water. To the best of my recollection I had never been there before. A bit depressed, I turned to read concern on Peter's face.

'Anything?'

'Nothing. I haven't the faintest idea why I should have spun off.' I looked round at the green and dun-coloured hills again but they inspired no memory. I shrugged.

'All right, Peter. Thanks for bringing me. It might have worked.'

As he started the car back south, Peter said amid the noisy step-function of changing gears: 'It may still come back. It certainly would be more satisfactory if we knew why you crashed. But I wouldn't worry. Life's full of untidy, unexplained loose ends. For example, one of our engineers just up and left us the other day without a word of explanation. He'd been here a year, seemed contented enough but can't have been. Of course, my mother would explain his behaviour as a simple example of the ingratitude of the lower orders. Ah. We turn off left here.'

We went down a side road, crossed the Conieglen Water and had entered the wood before I realised we were on the driveway to the David Campbell Neurological Institute.

We halted outside the main entrance. Peter glanced at his watch.

'Eleven. I think firstly to my office, and I'll see if I can rustle up some coffee.'

Seated under the window in an armchair, I watched Peter paper-knife open the envelopes on his desk after he had ordered coffee. He looked up.

'Nothing that can't wait.'

'If you leave them long enough they answer themselves.'

'A devious philosophy. In point of fact, there was no real urgency to come in here this morning but I thought it'd be easier to get you the things you wanted from here and anyway we can talk more freely.'

A girl in a green overall brought in the coffee. When we were both supplied with cups and biscuits, I said:

'I'm still not clear about this place. Is it a hospital of sorts?'

'Yes and no. It doesn't take the place of the cottage hospital—you were brought in simply because you chose to have your accident so near to it. But there are a number of patients. If I said that it was an experimental institute that would be more accurate but might be misleading.'

I thought vaguely of guinea pigs. Peter waved a tea-biscuit.

'It began of course with Gran's desire to keep Dad's name and work alive. Hence the name of the place. I don't really know in what direction it might have developed or whether it might not have got off the ground at all if the board her lawyers set up hadn't interested Philip Ebor in it.'

Philip Ebor. Peter observed my non-reaction.

'Not your line. Ebor made a name for himself as an authority on brain functions and disorders. He isn't exactly popular with the medical establishment since his approaches are seldom orthodox and I think they look on him as a bit of a rogue elephant. Even so, he's had some successes in fields they've left strictly alone—he's had his failures too!—and he's attracted quite a few researchers into his orbit although it's probably not all that advantageous to your career to say you've spent the past few years working with Philip Ebor.'

'And he's here?'

'Here, there and everywhere. He spends about one-third of his time here—he's Director—another third running his practice in London, and the rest of the time overseas. He's really a most remarkable man. He began life as an electronics man, made a successful living at it then got interested in EEG work and the insight it gives into the brain. He went to medical school, qualified and did a number of years staff work before branching out on his own.'

'I see.'

'There are laboratories here for experimental work with animals. And some of Ebor's long-term patients stay here.' He frowned. 'There are some pathetic cases—quite a few from road accidents'—I felt my scalp tighten—'but in many cases, Ebor seems to get results.' He got to his feet. 'Would you like to see something of this place?'

'I would.'

'Okay, we will now give you the sixty cents tour, strictly non-technical.' In the corridor, he added, 'Now remember, don't overdo it. If your ankle acts up, sing out.'

Actually, my ankle did seem a great deal improved and in any case I wanted to see more of the Institute.

To some extent it resembled all university or research institute scientific and technical departments with staff-rooms, their occupants' names and titles on the doors, two small lecture-rooms equipped with blackboards, screens and epidiascope, store-rooms for scientific and medical apparatus, and laboratories. One of the latter, seen from a corridor through a glass wall, seemed at first glance to contain a computer complex, with console display panels studded with multi-coloured light bulbs, and tape decks. There was also a print-out unit but instead of lines of letters and figures, a bank of pens had drawn wiggling, speedily-oscillating lines in jagged traces that strongly resembled the outputs from radio telescopes. There was also a couch with tables beside it festooned with tangles of wires and electrodes. Peter nodded sociably to a white-coated man working on the apparatus.

'The electroencephalograph room. I don't understand it but evidently by studying the electrical output from various parts of the brain you can learn quite a lot about the personality. Ebor has gone a bit further than most in this field. A lot of this EEG stuff he designed himself.'

We moved on.

The animal quarters were divided into two sections. One contained animals not taking part in experiments; the other was itself split by partitions into rooms holding test animals and any apparatus required for the particular experiments involved. For all the bright and airy conditions inside, there was the inevitable zoo smell of sawdust and ammonia and vegetables with a background noise of chirps, squeaks, chatterings and rustlings. The animals reacted to our presence characteristically; one rhesus monkey regarded us solemnly out of big eyes that seemed to mourn their owner's lack of understanding; his companion, apart from one quick, quizzical glance, continued to search his brown fur diligently. I looked into the first animal's eyes and thought again how often chimps and monkeys seem to be aware that their species just didn't quite make it in the intelligence stakes.

We passed into the second section. Many of the animals there had undergone brain surgery. Peter drew my attention to one row of cages, each of which contained a cat.

'They've got permanently-implanted microelectrodes in their brains. Quite painless. Ebor claims he can place electrodes in what he calls the pain, rage, fear, pleasure, hunger, thirst centres. That one, for example. The electrode was connected to a battery and a key and when the cat got the hang of it, it kept pressing the key and exhibiting the most intense pleasure for hour upon hour, even refusing food and drink. And that one there. Feed a little electricity to its microelectrode and instead of being a nice, placid tabby, it goes into a spitting, scratching fit of rage like a cornered Highland wildcat. Stop the current and Pussy Hyde becomes Dr Jekyll again.'

I had read of such experiments in science journals. But

being brought face to face with animals that had been tampered with, seeing their shaved fur, the scars of surgery plainly visible, produced mixed reactions. Mingled with admiration for the ingenious and daring research that was enlarging our understanding of the functions of the brain, there were the age-old qualms of conscience aroused by the exploitation of the animal kingdom by man. Yet rationally I could balance the immense amount of good achieved by brain surgeons in relieving human misery, armed with such experimentally-acquired knowledge, against the artificially-induced sufferings of these test animals. And a third factor I recognised was a primitive and superstitious reluctance to accept the implication of such experiments that man, one day, would be completely blueprinted, each cerebral circuit traced and understood.

The cat whose pleasure centre had been microelectroded yawned widely, revealing sharp white teeth and a long pink tongue. Instant ecstasy, I thought. Peter looked at his watch.

'Good heavens, half-past twelve. Let's get some lunch. How is your ankle?'

'It's okay,' I lied. Now that I attended to it, I realised it was burning. I made use of the stick when we left the animal quarters.

The moderately-sized staff dining-room with long, brightly-curtained windows contained four refectory tables. The wall on our left as we entered was given over to a self-service counter presided over by two white-overalled kitchen staff. Only two of the tables nearest the far side of the room were occupied.

'Saturday's quiet,' said Peter.

As we walked up to the counter, I noticed four people, three men and Dr Selkirk, seated at the table next to it. One of the men I recognised as Dr Preston; the other two I hadn't seen before. The only one facing us, a big, sandy-haired man in his late forties, with a strong, confident face, grinned in welcome at Peter and pointed inquiringly to the two unoccupied chairs beside him. Peter nodded. Because of my stick, he took the dishes I chose on to his own tray. I noted from his own ample selection that he was as fond of his food as ever.

I found myself seated between Peter and the sandy-haired man. Opposite the latter Dr Preston smiled and nodded. Peter distributed the dishes and performed introductions. The sandy-haired man was Philip Ebor; his firm handshake and the confident, yet warm look from grey eyes set in features that were almost classical Red Indian in their strength made me realise that only a man of his type, not so much arrogant as simply incapable of a failure of nerve, could carry on the kind of work he had chosen. Beside him, Dr Preston was a wisp; probably capable enough but a follower, a satellite.

The other man was more interesting. With thick, dark curly hair and a tanned complexion, an engaging humour lurking in deep brown eyes, he could have belonged to one of the Mediterranean races. When he laughed, his tan emphasised white, even teeth. Peter introduced him as Dr Ramon O'Keefe.

'And Dr Selkirk you know.'

She smiled. 'How are you, Dr Ramsay?'

'Much improved. This is a social visit.'

'Well, don't overdo it.' She turned to Ebor. 'Dr Ramsay is the person who selected our front door to have his motor accident outside.'

Ebor's deep voice was pleasantly modulated. 'Indeed. Yes, I heard about that.' His sandy head jerked towards Dr Selkirk. 'Did she patch you up satisfactorily?'

'Oh yes. No complaints.'

O'Keefe's brown eyes twinkled. 'I hear you are attached to the tracking station near here. Is it one of the American network?'

'No. Glasgow University. We collaborate on occasion with NASA.'

'NASA has a large station in my own country.'

'Where's that, Dr O'Keefe?'

'Armilla. Our island in the eastern Caribbean is very strategically placed for tracking manned spaceflight shots from Cape Kennedy.'

I looked at him with increased interest. One of the fellows I'd worked beside at Goddard Space Flight Center had spent a year at the Armilla station. From him I'd received a description of a tropical island set in a travel poster ocean, with a fecund, disease-ridden, semi-illiterate population of two million held in subjection by a devious life-term President and his thug army.

Jerry Colombo had spent a year in Armilla. He said that the ever-present realisation that the individual—any individual—was at the mercy of arrogant, psychopathic thugs without any moral or legal restraints produced a cumulative rasping of the nerves. The American group were by all rational estimates safe—they contributed a sizeable slice to the island's economy, apart from their nation's power, but rational considerations were alien to most of the President's strong-arm men. Lord Acton would have recognised the situation, or indeed anyone who had lived in Hitler's Germany or any of those other totalitarian regimes that have earned man the psychiatrist's description of 'the sick animal'.

In Jerry's case he had also had the ill-luck to fall in love with a girl there, an Armillan student who had been educated in Europe, had returned to the island and become involved in anti-government activities. When she disappeared, Jerry had, as an American diplomat put it, 'made a nuisance of himself' until, for his own protection, he had been flown home. I remembered his bleak, bitter face as he recalled the wall of fear, smiling insolence or veiled threats he had run into while he was searching for his girl.

A far cry from the sunlit Mull of Kintyre and this Institute and the civilised discussion of the practical benefits of spaceflight we conducted while these thoughts formed a dark counterpoint in my mind.

Ebor said: 'To my mind, if a fraction of the money had been put into brain research it would have been infinitely better spent. Our charts of the human brain are still like the early nineteenth century maps of Africa, a fringe of knowledge surrounding vast areas of ignorance or guesswork. What makes a man tick?—what is the physical basis of memory, of intelligence?—why does this man go paranoid?—and why do so many others slavishly follow him? Oh, there's so many questions to be answered, far more important than asking whether an American or a Russian will be first on the Moon.' He grinned. 'But then, I'm prejudiced.' He crumpled up the paper napkin he'd been using and rose.

'I've got to go now. Things to do. Nice meeting you, Dr Ramsay. Maybe some time you'll let me visit your station at Low Glenadale.'

I told him he'd be welcome and that we'd arrange something. Preston left with him, looking more than ever like his shadow. I wondered with a certain vague uneasiness if there was a cat or monkey somewhere waiting to have microelectrodes implanted in its brain. Then I realised Peter was speaking.

'Jane and Ramon are joining us tonight.'

O'Keefe's white teeth shone. 'I am looking forward to it. Your—what is her name?—Mrs Davenport sounds interesting. I shall compare her performance with that of the voodoo-dancers in my own country.' His eyes twinkled. 'Will there be drum-beating and the slaying of chickens and orgiastic dancing?'

Peter yelped with laughter. 'Oh no. My mother wouldn't approve. And you must promise to be serious.' He sobered. 'We've got to remember that Gran takes it all seriously.'

'Of course.' O'Keefe smiled. 'We shall be good. We promise, don't we, Jane?'

She returned the smile. 'We promise.'

Peter said to her, mock-seriously:

'Do you think Alan's fit enough to stay up for the show?'

She regarded me solemnly, her eyes glinting.

'Oh I think so. He seems to have a solid teak head.'

An hour later, we returned to Borgadel House. My ankle told me I'd better give it some time off so I rested on my bed while Peter prowled about my room and reminisced about old times.

A thought struck me.

'This chap I met, Dr O'Keefe. It's an Irish name, the same as the President of Armilla. Any relation?'

'Father and son. Family emigrated to Armilla a century ago during the hungry forties. They built up a fortune as merchants and landowners. Entered politics.'

'Yes, I know.' I told him about Jerry Colombo. Peter's mouth twisted.

'Nasty. I know how I'd react if I lost Alison in that way.' He swung round. 'But Ramon's all right. Studied medicine in the States, went back and ran a clinic in Ciudad Armilla, then met Ebor when he spent six months there as a visiting professor or something. He came back to the Institute for a year's research work with Philip. He's a most entertaining character. Very bright indeed. In the year he's been here his English, which was strongly American and not too good, has become almost perfect and he's quite lost the American accent.'

He grinned. 'You haven't met Gonzales yet, have you? Gonzales is ostensibly Ramon's chauffeur. Really I think he is supposed to be a bodyguard in case any of the Armillan underground try to kidnap him. The whole thing's ridiculous, of course. Apart from Ramon being extremely popular at home, from what Philip tells me, the idea of Armillan revolutionaries skulking about the Mull of Kintyre induces mind-boggling at a high rate of knots. Anyway, Ramon adopts a very lighthearted attitude to it all, which is why Gonzales goes about with a permanently worried expression. He knows he'd end up in Papa O'Keefe's cellars if anything happened to Ramon.'

Abruptly I remembered the snatch of conversation I had overheard from the summerhouse on the cliff top. I told Peter. He stared at me, his head cocked to one side.

'How extraordinary.' He rubbed his chin. 'Are you sure?'

'Yes.'

'I mean, you say you had almost fallen asleep. It's sometimes difficult to distinguish fact from fantasy in such circumstances.'

'Yes, I know. But I'm pretty certain.'

He turned away towards the curtained window so that his face was hidden.

'Extraordinary,' he repeated. 'And you didn't recognise the voices?'

'No.'

'Well, look,' he said, 'what shall we do?'

I hesitated. The thought of phoning someone and saying in so many words, 'Sorry to trouble you, old chap, but I think I've just overheard what might be a discussion about kidnapping you' invoked a confused embarrassment I shied away from. And yet if there was the slightest possibility . . .

'I think I would phone now,' I said.

Peter sighed. He stalled a little but a minute or so later he gave in and left the bedroom. When he returned he grinned sheepishly.

'I told Ramon. He asked me to thank you but was so solemn about it I know he was laughing like a drain. Oh well, duty done.'

I nodded. Inwardly I felt dissatisfied in a nebulous sort of way. My nagging sense of missing something intensified. I found I was looking fixedly at Peter and shrugged.

5 . . . And a stirring of echoes

We had sherry in the sitting-room before dinner while we awaited the arrival of O'Keefe and Jane Selkirk. O'Keefe, his dark, well-cut suit, his tan and dark hair contrasting with his white shirt-cuffs and teeth, was obviously out to enjoy himself. More and more, he seemed to epitomise the international man, at home in every civilised community, not because of any chameleon-like quality of character, for he would always register positively, unlike Dr. Preston. He had a natural charm and ease of conversation that as a rather dour Scot I admired without envy and I found myself warming to him.

Jane Selkirk arrived ten minutes after O'Keefe. She halted just inside the lounge door, accepted a glass of sherry from Peter, smiled and moved towards the log fire. She wore an evening frock in an almost cobalt shade of blue; the only jewelry she wore was a double strand of pearls.

I had been talking to Dorothy West, enjoying her slightly astringent wit and I found the contrast between the two women intriguing. Mrs West, skilfully made up, her own dark hair drawn back to the crown of her head in what appeared to be her favourite hairstyle, was unquestionably attractive. Perhaps part of her attraction for me was her obvious insight into men's minds, her almost amused air with them and, I supposed, my knowledge of her past influence on Peter. Jane Selkirk, as we talked, gave the impression of friendliness, of quiet confidence and, well, of niceness—an overworked and misused word but somehow appropriate. Yet there was nothing obvious or shallow about her; without putting on a mask there was a self-possession that suggested a deep, well-integrated personality, utterly feminine and with just that degree of mystery that many attractive women have.

'Who's minding the shop?' I asked.

'Dr Preston. He'll cope.'

Out of the corner of my eye while we talked, I observed the others. Alison and Peter, over by the drinks table, were talking to O'Keefe. A burst of appreciative laughter acknowledged one of his remarks.

A maid came to the door and caught Dorothy West's eye. She crossed, listened, then announced that dinner was ready. We trooped through, Jane Selkirk being placed on my left with Dorothy West on my right. Opposite me Alison sat beside O'Keefe. Peter took the head of the table; his mother the foot.

While soup was being served, Peter told us that his grandmother was having a light dinner in her room; Mrs. Davenport, too, would join us after dinner in the library.

The conversation therefore was more lighthearted than it would have been and the little dinner party passed by very pleasantly. Inevitably the subject of spiritualism came up. Ramon described the ceremonies he had witnessed in Armilla; they seemed to have strong affinities with similar voodoo practices on the neighbouring island of Haiti.

'They still hold the population in thrall,' he said ruefully. 'Love potions, curses, philtres against sterility—as if we needed those!—horoscopes.'

'Have you anything analogous to zombies?' I asked.

O'Keefe sobered. 'It is said that in the remoter and more primitive areas of the country you can see those creatures working in the fields, empty shells of human beings, no soul, just half-dead, half-alive husks of humanity.'

Margaret Campbell spoke sharply:

'But Dr O'Keefe, surely that's mere superstitious rubbish.'

Ramon tilted his head slightly. 'I've never seen them,' he admitted. 'But can we say they cannot exist? Surely it is possible that there are drugs that destroy the higher faculties, those that make up the essential essence of personality and yet do not kill the body though they appear to do so. And have you never carried out a complicated series of actions quite automatically because your mind was elsewhere?'

'A bit like the politician,' Peter put in, 'who dreamed he was giving a speech in the House and woke up to find he was!'

'Exactly.' Ramon grinned. 'However, whether such drugs exist in Armilla or not, I do not know. What I do know is that my country, for all it has universities and is part of the American Space Tracking Network, is still largely a land of primitive superstition.' And a howling dictatorship, I added privately. Ramon continued. 'But we do make progress. For the first time most of the educated class possess television sets and we run our own TV network.'

He smiled disarmingly. 'Now, I know the staple diet of programmes is mostly westerns and soap operas but they are the sugar coatings for the educational programme pills we slip in.' He sighed. 'It's a slow process. I'm afraid the voodoo priest will still be with us for a long time to come.'

I had a sudden surrealist vision of an Armillan TV commercial where a bizarrely-dressed announcer plugged the fabulously successful qualities of Mama Legba's potion for producing zombies.

By coffee-time, Peter, much to my surprise, had persuaded his mother to join us in the library. I suppose curiosity tipped the balance. It had been interesting while we discussed psychical research and spiritualism to hear the company's views. None was a spiritualist; all, except Peter's mother, unshaken in her citadel of dogma, admitted ignorance about the subjects but claimed to be open-minded.

'What about you, Alan?' Jane asked.

'I think extrasensory perception has been proved to exist. I think the world is infinitely more complicated than we imagine.'

'I knew a man once,' Peter said, 'who believed only he

existed. Everything else, people, trees, sun, moon and stars were figments of his imagination.'

'Solipsism,' O'Keefe stated. 'Logically unassailable, emotionally unsatisfactory.'

I nodded. 'Yes. When I was a student I used to long for a way of avoiding the necessary assumption that the world isn't a figment of my imagination.' I looked round the table. 'I never found one.'

Ramon laughed. 'Don't wake him, Jane. He's dreaming us and if you wake him we'll all disappear.'

I looked at Jane and thought: I couldn't dream of a nicer person.

'Time's a'going,' Peter said. 'I think we'd better move into the library. Dorothy, would you like to let Gran and Mrs Davenport know we've assembled?'

In preparation for the seance a fire had been lit in the library. Its red-hot coals now resembled glowing charcoal in a watchman's brazier and the room was almost too warm. The plum-coloured velvet curtains had been drawn; the doors on either side of the fireplace were shut. Around the heavy oval table the chairs waited. On a small side-table stood the Philips tape-recorder produced by Peter earlier that afternoon.

We stood around, the heightening of tension betrayed by too loud remarks or laughs, like students before they're allowed into the examination hall. Peter recalled that he had read somewhere that even the Russians, contrary to Marxist materialism, were becoming interested in psychical research and I told them of a cartoon I had seen in *Punch* where four irate Russian colonels were shown seated around a table strewn with alphabet cards, their forefingers on an upturned tumbler, their eyes fixed exasperatedly upwards, the caption being 'Ve have vays of making you talk!' The laughter died when old Mrs Campbell entered the room, followed by Mrs Davenport and Dorothy West. The housekeeper closed the door.

Mrs Davenport wore a long black evening dress with a touch of white lace at the neck. She was very much in charge of the proceedings. Her chin slightly raised, she surveyed the circle.

'I think we will have the lights out. There will be sufficient light from the fire. No, Mrs West, don't put them out until we're seated.'

Peter glanced at me.

'Mrs Davenport, I wonder if you'd have any objection to us taping the seance.' He indicated the recorder.

Mrs Davenport smiled indulgently. 'Not at all.'

'What about you, Gran?'

Old Mrs Campbell's breathy voice revealed her enhanced emotional state.

'Please do, Peter. It would be nice to have a record. We should have thought of it for the earlier sittings.'

So we should, I told myself, my mood hardening.

Two minutes later, we were sitting round the polished table. The mike had been placed on one of the shelves, the recorder switched on. I watched the spools lazily turning, the brown magnetic oxide coated tape threading through the recording head. At Mrs Davenport's request, Dorothy had switched off the lights before taking her place on my right. In fact, as my eyes accommodated themselves to the red firelight, I saw that by chance or some slight hangover from the dinner table, we had taken up essentially the same seating arrangements, except that at the end of the short axis of the elliptical table, Mrs Davenport sat between Alison and O'Keefe while Peter's grandmother sat beside him at the long end of the table on my left. Because of this, Alison, Mrs Davenport and O'Keefe were opposite me, their backs to the firelight, a red corona outlining the eclipsing black bulk of the medium.

'We will sit quietly for a while to allow our minds to settle and the power to build. During this time I will receive impressions from spirit and will possibly be able to transmit messages from those dear ones outside the body. At the right time I will go into trance.' A chair creaked as someone shifted—on my right? 'My control will take over—he is a John Edwards, a young Methodist minister who died about 1896 of typhoid just at the beginning of his ministry—very sad. However he now carries on his work on a higher plane helping to unite those still in the body with those loved ones outwith it.' I darted a glance to left and right. I had no difficulty in the firelight in seeing my companions' faces. I could read nothing from Jane's; I thought I did detect an almost delighted 'Is it possible!' glint in Dorothy West's eye. The faces of those opposite me were in shadow.

'Do not be alarmed by anything you see or hear. If any communicator is heard or addresses you, you may reply. It often helps the spirit to establish a link. Now, will you all join hands? Remember, we act as a sort of galvanic battery of power to be drawn upon by those in spirit. But also remember! Do not expect too much, sometimes the conditions are not suitable.'

In the general rustle of clothing and creaking of chairs, I thought: she has all the jargon, including the escape clause; makes it sound business-like and persuasive to the impressionable, creates just the right expectant atmosphere in which the average person will be even more of an unreliable witness than he usually is. I felt Jane's cool fingers in my left hand, Dorothy's warmer grasp in my right. On an impulse I squeezed the latter's fingers; she squeezed back, her mouth giving the merest twitch of amused acknowledgement.

Silence except for the chesty breathing of old Mrs Campbell.

Someone clears their throat; the dignified ticking of the clock on the mantelpiece measures off the seconds. Minutes pass. Then a knock, as if someone raps a knuckle once on the table. A sigh from a sitter—Alison?—more raps, a gasping snort from Margaret Campbell almost reminiscent of a bridling horse. Mrs Davenport's light conversational tones.

'Ah, I am getting impressions. There are a number of friends in spirit here. Yes, dear, I hear you. Yes, I—What's that? Yes, yes.' There followed the usual mixture of cryptic statements, of vague descriptions of men and women on the other side claimed by Mrs Davenport to be dead relations and friends of the sitters, of name-fishing, eager grasping by the medium at tentative, doubtful acknowledgements by members of the circle wishing out of sheer good manners to be helpful, more rappings, impossible to localise in the dim orange-red illumination, the table creaking as if about to tilt, then Mrs Davenport once more.

'I think the time has come for me to enter the trance state. The power is building up nicely. Remember, on no account disturb me while in trance.'

I eased my position, conscious that in spite of my complete scepticism, I was tense. My head, for the first time that day, ached slightly. Dorothy leaned towards me. In my ear she breathed, 'My nose is itchy.'

I whispered, 'Poltergeists, I presume,' and steered her left hand to her nose.

'Thanks.'

Mrs Davenport was well under by now, huddled bulkily in her chair, her breathing through pursed mouth a vibrant, snoring susurration. It could well have been genuine, I thought. Suddenly she straightened up. The voice of a young man, north of England accent, quite unlike her own, came cheerfully and strongly from her lips.

'Good evening, friends. I am John Edwards. I welcome you on behalf of our spirit friends to this meeting. Conditions are not good tonight but perhaps we may achieve something . . .'

As the platitudes and spiritual uplift rambled on I wondered: secondary personality? I couldn't be sure. Edwards continued:

'There are two men here who have been different lengths of time out of the body.' There followed a recognisable description of Mrs Campbell's sons and I was reminded of the two wax dummies sitting beyond the closed door to the left of the fireplace. My uneasiness and distaste grew as the old lady's breathing quickened and deepened. Edwards said he was now asked to tell their mother they were happy together as well as their father—very busy in the spirit world and they would try to communicate more directly now that contact had been made.

There followed a number of supposed proofs that the alleged communicators were really who they professed to be—events from their childhood, Colin spending a whole summer just before the war building the fir-cone summer-house after a trip to the Black Forest—'it's a pity to see it so dilapidated now, Mother'—'glad you've kept father's old car museum; do you remember how the Arrol-Johnson came to pieces ten yards past the post after winning the old car rally?'

It was all done very convincingly, with Edwards conducting his conversation with the two unseen brothers and relaying their remarks to the sitters. Yet I knew that it was entirely possible the medium was dredging all the data from the minds of the sitters before dramatising it, in much the same way, perhaps, dream-characters are made to walk the boards of our mental theatres when we sleep.

And then I found myself catching my breath.

Even while Edwards continued to trundle out his hotch-potch of religious aphorisms, I heard whispers, soft, almost inaudible, but definitely present. Jane's fingers tightened on mine, O'Keefe stirred, cocking his head as if trying to hear them better. The control's voice died away as the whispers became louder. The medium's head slumped forward. Straining my ears, I began to hear phrases.

'. . . difficult, very difficult. Perhaps better next time. . . . Must keep trying. . . . This is Colin, Mother . . . David's with me. . . .'

'It is Colin—it is Colin!' The old lady's breathing was even faster, even more laboured, though I was sure the whispering voice could have been anyone's. The medium moaned and writhed as if in nightmare. From the edge of the table in front of her a twisting coil of white mist rose against the blackness of her dress, then tinged with pink when the firelight caught it. Under her breath I heard Dorothy whisper 'Oh God!' while Peter half-rose from his chair.

'Keep still,' I said sharply. 'Don't break the circle.'

The smokiness seemed to pulsate as if trying to find a shape then it began to disperse, spilling off the table edge like mist over the brow of a mountain. A last, almost despairing murmur '. . . too difficult', was followed by mutterings that died away as the mist finally vanished. I became conscious of Jane's fingernails burning the palm of my left hand like acid, was turning my head towards her when fresh phenomena began.

For a moment I was unable to locate the sobs, gusty, struggling cries as if someone fought in a frenzy of terror for their life then I saw that they came from Alison. From her mouth, opening and closing convulsively, a voice in deep distress issued, its urgency holding us in a frozen tableau. I strove to register the words.

'. . . the world's going—it's shattered. I see the sounds. I see them. Car. I am in his car. Oh God! The water's cold. I can't breathe. Help me! He-l-p me! I'm drowning. They're poisoning their minds. Stop them. Stop them!'

As the voice rose to a scream, Peter sprang to Alison's side, his chair crashing back.

'Alison! Alison! It's all right.' Over his shoulder he shouted: 'Get the lights on.'

With no conscious act of volition I found myself at the light switch. I brushed Dorothy West's hand aside.

'Not yet,' I said. 'There's light enough. The medium's still in trance and Alison's coming out of it.'

And indeed she was quieter now though great sobs still shook her in Peter's arms. O'Keefe stood on the other side of Mrs Davenport, who showed signs of coming out of trance. Jane was moving round the table towards Alison; the others sat in stunned silence. While Dorothy stared up at me in puzzlement, I watched the medium. She stood up, looking completely disorientated.

'Get those lights on, for God's sake,' Peter cried, his voice betraying fury and fear. I judged that no harm would be done.

Peter swung round on me.

'What the hell were you waiting for?' he snarled.

'Till both were out of it.'

'Both?' His anger turned to bewilderment.

'Yes. Alison went under too.'

His gaze dropped to her, lying huddled against him, her body still wrenched by sobs. On Jane's instruction, Dorothy left the library to fetch brandy. Even O'Keefe, I noticed, seemed shaken. Old Mrs Campbell, flushed and distressed, lay back in her chair, an odd mixture of grief and yearning on her face. Her daughter-in-law's features registered outraged fear and anger. She muttered something; I think it was 'Hysterical nonsense!' but her hand on the back of the old lady's chair shook uncontrollably. Mrs Davenport's flamboyant appearance had a crumpled, bewildered look about it now; the events had shaken her too, I was certain.

'You're all right,' Peter insisted. Alison rubbed her forehead with the tips of her fingers, her head moving from one side to the other, the light glinting off her fair hair; again I thought how frail she looked.

'I'm all right.' Her voice shook and she drew in a gasping breath. 'Oh God! I don't want that again.' She took the brandy glass from Dorothy, drank—I could hear her teeth rattle on the edge of it—grimaced and handed it to Peter.

'Someone or something tried to invade my mind—to push me out.' She shivered. 'I found myself fighting for my very existence. The horrible thing was that he was terrified too.' Quite suddenly she broke down, gasping, weeping, while Peter comforted her, murmuring those idiotic phrases we use at such moments. A sort of psychic rape, I thought. I caught Jane's eye. As if by mutual consent we turned away from the others.

'Have you seen this kind of thing before?' she asked.

'No. Though I've heard of it.'

She regarded me thoughtfully. 'I somehow gathered the impression you were familiar with such things.'

'I've been to seances before. I used to go a lot when I was a student. I read a lot too.'

The hazel eyes held mine while her head tilted very slightly in Alison's direction.

'It could be hysterics but I don't think so. But if it isn't . . .'

I nodded. 'A bit disturbing.'

'Yes.' She frowned. 'What about all the other things, the raps, the creaks, the voices, all that information—and that white substance? Is that what they call ectoplasm?'

I grinned wryly. 'I don't attach any weight to those.' I lowered my voice. 'Any fraudulent medium worth her salt could put on such a show. Remember—she's had two previous sessions with the old lady to fish for information.

And that outfit she's got on could conceal a complete conjuror's cabinet. She could have a tapper strapped to the underside of her thigh and I wouldn't be surprised if that mist was carbon dioxide gas subliming from a small dry ice container she'd brought down with her in a Thermos.'

'And the voices?'

'Have you seen the way they're miniaturising taperecorders these days? I've seen some used in artificial satellites smaller than cigarette packets.'

Her eyes glinted. 'What a nasty suspicious mind you have.'

'So everyone tells me.' I turned to hear what the others were saying. Old Mrs Campbell was patting Alison's shoulder.

'. . . if I'd known it would end like this, my dear, I wouldn't have started it. Oh, I'm very grateful to you, Mrs Davenport, for your help. You have helped. My sons were here. I feel sure of that and I'm sure I heard Colin's voice.' She hesitated. 'Perhaps, some time in the future . . .' She broke off and I turned away and caught Jane's compassionate expression. She glanced at me and her mouth twisted. I thought I knew what she was thinking. Mrs Davenport, her ebullience somewhat restored, bestowed her white smile on the company, a brave smile, one that spoke of the expenditure of valuable psychic energy in the interests of truth.

'Thank you, Mrs Campbell.' She sighed. 'Sometimes we do encounter wicked, sick spirits. And sometimes they don't fasten on to the medium whose control is well capable of dealing with them'—slap them on their psychic wrist and send them packing, I thought—'but they seize upon a member of the circle who happens to be sensitive—but inexperienced. Even though in spirit, they are not reconciled to their lot but still seek earthly experience with a desperate greediness.' She addressed Alison. 'And you *are* sensitive, my dear. There's no doubt about that. You must decide whether you are going to develop your talent—it is a gift beyond price though it bears tremendous responsibilities and burdens'—she sighed again just to make sure we appreciated that she knew—'or let it sleep. It is up to you.'

Looking at Alison's white, strained face, I thought it a safe bet that the last thing she desired was a repetition of the experience. The Davenport prepared to make her exit.

'And now, if you don't mind, I shall leave you. I find these seances, especially where results *have* been achieved, rather exhausting. If I could have a glass of hot milk in fifteen minutes time in my room.'

'I'll bring it to you,' Dorothy promised. She addressed the company. 'There's coffee in the lounge.' Mrs Campbell senior said she would also go up to bed; her daughter-in-law went to assist her. I hoped Margaret Campbell wouldn't seize the opportunity to work on the old lady. The soft flapping of the tape end told me the recorder was still on and I crossed to it and switched it off. Peter, Alison and O'Keefe followed the others out; I was half aware that Jane Selkirk still stood by the door. Just for the record's sake, I mooched about the room, noting that the tiny pieces of Sellotape and the lengths of black thread I had used to seal the fireplace doors and the windows were intact. By the nature of the seance, it didn't really matter but in other circumstances it might have been helpful.

'You're limping,' Jane accused.

'Guilty.' I returned to my place at the oval table, righting Peter's overturned chair en route. Stooping, I retrieved my stick.

'You've been on your feet far too much.'

'Guilty, guilty, guilty.' I approached her, craftily concealing my limp.

'Honestly, you great, strong, manly men! Can't acccept your limitations. I don't know why we bother patching you up.'

'Very good of you.'

'How's your head?'

'Fine,' I lied.

'You need a nanny. I should have kept you in the Institute another three days at least.'

Her anger was engaging, the dark, frowning eyebrows something that made me feel absurdly lighthearted. I crossed my heart and raised my right hand solemnly.

'I solemnly swear that Sunday shall be a day of rest for

Alan Ramsay.' I added hesitantly: 'Of course, if you happened to have some time off, say tomorrow afternoon and hadn't anything better to do, you could keep an eye on me, you know, just to make sure I didn't go for a long hike all over the Mull of Kintyre.'

Her eyes speculative, she looked at me. 'It so happens I am off tomorrow afternoon.' It was her turn to hesitate. 'Peter was saying you haven't seen much of the Mull?'

'No. That is, I haven't. I've been in the li'l old USA for the past three years.'

'All right, I'll give you a conducted tour by car.'

'Yes please.'

'I'll call for you at two-thirty. Will that do?'

'Fine. Now, perhaps we'd better join the others before they think the spooks have got us.'

I followed her from the library across the hall, listening to her heels clicking on the tiled floor, my eyes on the dark lustrous crown of her head. I felt a tingling, glowing feeling of excitement that overwhelmed my various aches and pains, dismissing for a time the disturbed, uneasy mood the seance had produced.

In the big lounge fireplace, fresh logs were blazing, spitting out their firework display of sparks. Alison, coffee cup in hand, was huddled in a corner of a couch, gazing chillily into the fire. Peter carried a whisky glass across and sat beside her. He took her free hand in his: she smiled quickly at him. O'Keefe, before the fire, turned towards us.

'Ah, there you are. Have some coffee, or'—he raised his own glass—'something stronger, if you feel the need for it.'

I accepted black coffee from Jane, took a mouthful of the hot tangy liquid and caught sight of the grandfather clock. It registered eleven-fifteen. Outside the uncurtained windows darkness lay over the hills of the Mull, the grounds of the house black except where the room lights splashed harshly against lawn and bushes. By unspoken agreement, none of us talked about the seance in detail, though I wanted quite badly to question Alison about her experience and ask Peter to clear up some matters. But I thought things could wait until morning. In fact we talked round the evening's events rather than about them, Dorothy joining us when she had taken the Davenport her nightcap.

O'Keefe and Jane left twenty minutes later. We stood at the main door while their cars swung down the drive through the pitchy canyon of undergrowth then we turned indoors. We said goodnight to one another in subdued tones.

Strangely enough, I slept easily, wakening fresh and alert at a quarter to eight. I shaved and washed, noting with satisfaction that an early morning heat haze promised a fine day. Realising I had an hour to wait for breakfast, I remembered the tape we'd made of the seance and thought I'd play it over. In the library, I pulled back the heavy curtains to admit the sunshine. I stood for a moment gazing at the oval table and its chairs, recalling the previous night's events then crossed to the recorder. I rewound the tape on to the left-hand reel, stabbed the replay key and began to sample until I found Mrs Davenport's instructional speech to the sitters.

I listened for a minute, was just about to skip forward again when her voice halted in mid-sentence as if guillotined, to be replaced by the feather-soft hiss of the tape inching through the head. I stopped the machine, rewound and tried again. But it was no use. Ten minutes further sampling confirmed that the seance record had been wiped from the tape. For a long moment I stood there looking stupidly at the tape-recorder before the angry squeaks of two sparrows squabbling outside the library window recalled me to my surroundings. I stopped gnawing my thumb-nail and went slowly and thoughtfully back to my bedroom.

6 Full of deadly poison

It was some time after breakfast that I had an opportunity to speak to Peter alone. We walked down to the fir-cone summerhouse and sat on the bench beside it facing the sea. The easy hum of insects and the sun-sparkled sea stretched out before us formed an incongruous background to our talk. I pushed the metal ferrule of my stick into the turf and listened to him denying any knowledge of the wiped tape. He seemed as perplexed as I was.

'It seems a senseless thing to do,' he said.

'But deliberate. You have to rewind, then begin recording silence, then stop the tape when it runs out.'

He plucked a twig from the rhododendron bush beside him and began stripping it of the fat, glossy leaves one by one, his plumpish face unusually serious.

'Do you know how your uncle Colin died?' I asked.

He gave me a startled glance.

'He was killed during the war. Didn't I tell you?'

'Yes. But how?'

'He went down in the *Lancastria*.'

In my mind I heard again the terrified voice from Alison's lips. Almost as if he caught an echo, Peter's eyes widened.

'Oh no! That voice last night. You're surely not suggesting . . .' He shook his head. 'I refuse to believe it. After all those years.'

'Well, your grandmother was trying to contact her sons.'

'No. I don't believe it. I'm sure there's some rational explanation. That woman Davenport is as phoney as a four-pound note. Surely you can see that.'

'Very likely. But what about Alison?'

He hesitated, frowned, then threw away the mutilated twig.

'She was carried away by the atmosphere. It was all pretty unnerving. That mist. . . . And she's pretty impressionable, highly-strung. Maybe even a sort of self-hypnosis.'

I listened to him rationalising it all away. Far out beyond Sanda Isle a small yacht made slow progress over the sea as if conscious it shouldn't be out on the Sabbath.

'Why scrub the tape? And what's more, when was it done?'

He shook his head irritably.

'I don't know. Sometime last night or very early this morning. It could be . . .'

He broke off and I wondered if he was thinking of all the people in Borgadel House, trying them in turn in the part of the tape-wiper. I had already done that without success.

'I'll ask Alison and Dorothy about it later,' he said. 'Anyway we seem to have made a right muck of the matter. Gran is convinced Mrs Davenport can tune in to the next world any time she pleases.' He took a thin silver cigarette case from his pocket. The sunlight flashed dazzlingly from it and I screwed my eyes up in reflex action. He smoked moodily for a minute, the bluish smoke dispersing lazily in the still air. It reminded me of Mrs Davenport's 'ectoplasm'. 'I don't know what else we can do.' He ground the cigarette into the turf and glanced at his watch. 'Come on, time to get ready for church.'

Qualms about being anti-social had made me accept old Mrs Campbell's invitation after breakfast to accompany her to church. Peter and Alison went in the Vauxhall Viva; I felt obliged to travel with the old lady and her daughter-in-law. Evidently Mrs Davenport wanted to rest after her labours to raise a world to life.

We waited in the hall for Mitchell to bring the car round. Mrs Campbell, her plump body swathed in black, bore an even closer resemblance to Queen Victoria in her later years. Her daughter-in-law, taller and wearing a grey coat and hat, carried a black glossy leather bible and hymn book. I was a little conscious of my unpressed flannels and elbow-patched sports jacket but consoled myself with the thought that in the sight of the Almighty we are all equal.

The car was a splendidly douce 1936 Rolls-Royce. I waited until the grey-uniformed chauffeur came round, opened the door, armed the old lady on to the ribbed running board and into the rear compartment. Margaret Campbell followed her then I took my place on the collapsible seat, my back to the windowed partition separating the passengers from the driver. The engine murmured smoothly and we moved off down the drive, gravel crunching under the huge tyres. Through the small back window, I watched the house recede.

'The church we're going to,' said the old lady, 'is the one I first went to as a child sixty-nine years ago.'

The ancient Rolls took us down the winding road then slowed at the junction where the road to Port Mean dived off steeply to the right. Looking out of the square side window I saw the outlying Port cottages, small, neat, clean, their painted doors breaking their whitewashed stonework, then the occasional shop with tiny cluttered window. Finally I got my first glimpse of the harbour, its wall made of great sandstone blocks sheltering an inner basin on which fishing boats floated.

Mitchell turned the Rolls down a side street, past a wide green over which groups of Sunday-suited people walked and finally drew us up before the plainly-built church. The single bell in the church tower clanged abruptly at second intervals, its confident sound and the scene before me reminding me again that it was the Scottish Sabbath and that in thousands of small communities all over the islands and highlands and lowlands of Scotland, worship in a supposedly secular age still followed closely the traditions of past centuries.

An elder welcomed us and conducted us to the Campbell pew halfway down the well-filled church, increasing my illusion of the Queen attending worship at Crathie. Once seated, I glanced around. The men in the congregation invariably wore dark suits, their hair, usually short back and sides, scrubbed into order, their out-door life evident in the permanent beaten tan of their faces. The women's and children's clothes provided random splashes of colour. I amused myself trying to pick out the small contingent of holiday-makers. The organ began to play softly, the church officer in his rusty black gown carried the big Bible up to the pulpit, came down and ushered in the minister with the proper solemnity and the service began.

Quite frankly, I had intended to think during the next hour, shutting off all of my attention except the fraction required to keep track of the congregation's responses to the ministerial commands 'Let us now sing to God's praise . . .', 'Let us now unite in prayer' and this I managed, like one of Ramon's zombies, until the sermon began. The New Testament lesson had been taken from Chapter 3 of James' epistle but I had been puzzling over the previous night's events and hadn't paid much attention. The elderly minister now chose as his text verse 8: 'But the tongue can no man tame; it is an unruly evil, full of deadly poison.' The minister paused, repeated the text, closed the book and gazed round the congregation. He seemed reluctant to begin, took a deep breath, smoothed down quite unnecessarily the starched white Geneva bands at his neck before speaking again. I was suddenly aware that a distinctly uneasy aura lay over the rows of attentive faces.

'Men and women, those holidaymakers present in our midst must forgive me if my address is sombre today. But recent tragic events in Port Mean have brought home to me the bitter necessity for this sermon. Indeed guilt lies heavy upon my conscience that I have not had the courage to speak before. . . .'

It was really an extraordinarily uncomfortable sermon. Even as a stranger, I felt the bite of the minister's words.

Apparently the little seaport in past months had been racked by a series of vicious rumours. All small communities have their bush-telegraph and most members of such villages or seaports could, if forced to, compile pretty detailed dossiers on their neighbours. This is not a bad thing. Much of the strength and character and endurance of such communities springs from this intimate, family knowledge of one's fellows.

In this case, however, as far as I could make out, the normal stream of gossip had burst its banks in a damaging torrent. Irresponsible rumours had been sweeping the Port, false alarms concerning the safety of fishing boats had caused distress, meaty statements imputing quite outrageous moral lapses to a number of the inhabitants had circulated so that a malaise of fear, distrust and hatred had gripped the few hundred inhabitants like a deep-seated virus infection. And now, in this past week, evidently, a young man had viciously assaulted a neighbour and a girl had committed suicide.

The old minister, behind his scathing denunciation, was hurt and perplexed. I watched the congregation's faces. Holidaymakers showed bewilderment and distaste, as if overhearing a family quarrel; shame, guilt, resentment and distress were the dominant expressions on the faces of the inhabitants. I saw at least two women weep. Peter told me afterwards that the Reverend Martin McAllister had been over forty years in Port Mean and had baptised most of those present. I thought back to his drawn, weary face and realised a little of what he had gone through to deliver that public rebuke.

Standing on the gravel path outside the church, I watched the family groups crossing the green. Down in the harbour, the ranks of bright-painted fishing boats—*Sea Spray, Ocean Harvest, Mona, Belle Star,* etc.—waited for the stroke of midnight, the fiducial mark separating the Lord's day from the first fishing day of the week.

When I told them at lunch that Jane Selkirk was collecting me at two-thirty, I expected, and got, some clever remarks from Peter.

'Well,' he said, 'I call that therapy beyond the call of

duty.' He winked at Alison. 'Are you sure you wouldn't like us to come along as additional guides? We know every inch of the geography of the Mull of Kintyre. Jane's a comparative newcomer to these parts; she might lead you astray.'

'I'll take my chance.' Afraid I had sounded stuffy, I asked: 'What are you going to do?'

'As if you cared.' He grinned. 'We'll probably spend the afternoon on the beach. It promises to be a scorcher.' I thought that Alison could do with a lazy afternoon in the sunshine; judging by the shadows below her eyes she hadn't slept much the previous night. Mrs Davenport wiped her red mouth with her napkin, an indulgent 'Ah! Youth, youth!' expression on her plump face.

I was sitting on the sun-warmed window-seat at the lounge oriel window reading the *Scottish Sunday Express* when Jane's pale blue Hillman Imp appeared in the drive. A news item about Armilla had caught my attention. An attempt to bomb the President using a modified air freighter had come to grief with the forced landing of the plane outside the capital, after three bombs had been dropped. One of them, a dud, had narrowly missed the President's personal escape plane, a big Cleat Tupolev TU-114 presented by the Russians some years back when O'Keefe was playing footsie with the Bear. The President's men, on information received from the captured crew, were in pursuit of the ringleaders, said to be agents of a foreign power. I tossed the paper aside. It appeared that Ramon's dear old dad was still firmly in the saddle.

Once in the front seat of the car, I put on my sunglasses. The early morning's promise of a really hot day had been kept. I looked at Jane while she got the Imp under way. She also wore sunglasses. The short-skirted cream, linen frock she had on left neck and arms and nicely-rounded knees bare. Not at all one's idea of a gruff old family doctor, I thought. I leaned back, feeling elated and one hundred per cent alive.

'I don't do this for all my patients,' she said, unconsciously paraphrasing Peter's remark.

'I know. Only the stupid ones with little pointed heads

who won't take care of themselves.'

She grinned, concentrating on guiding the car round bushy corners in the winding drive.

'What did you do this morning?' she asked.

'Went to church. You know, when in Rome do as the Romans do.'

'Not the most suitable phrase for a Church of Scotland household.'

I told her about the minister's sermon. She listened without interrupting.

'Strange business.' She turned left at the lodge gates. 'I don't live in Port Mean—I have a house near Carskiey—but I quite often go down to the Port. I like the people—they're honest and hardworking and kind—oh, I know some of them get drunk and there is the loutish minority and the odd one knocks his wife about and quarrels arise—but it's a good community. They're still more dependent on fishing than on holidaymakers.' She put on a Highland accent. 'The herring iss a great, great mystery. The more you will be catchin' of them the more there iss; and when they're no' in't at all they're no' there.' She giggled. 'Para Handy.'

I nodded. 'There aren't many of these fishing villages left.'

'Port Mean didn't even have television until a year or so ago. Something to do with the circle of hills and cliffs preventing reception. Then old Mrs Campbell had a repeater or booster station built on the hill between Borgadel House and the Port to catch the programmes and pipe them down into the village.'

'Yes, I saw the mast in the grounds.'

The car was climbing, travelling almost due west between highlands that must have topped the 1,200 mark. It was hill-sheep country, bleak, rocky but with a thick carpet of gorse, heather, tough grass, bog cotton and wild flowers all producing their own fragrance. Down to the left of the narrow single track, a stream drained the hillsides. The climb continued until we came to a broad parking area between two hills. Beyond the parking area the road dropped in swooping banking turns and I noticed a warning to motorists suggesting that they took their cars no further.

'Think you can stagger fifty yards? The view is worth it.'

'I think so.'

We got out and I used my stick to help me over the springy turf. Beyond the Gap, as Jane called it, the land fell sharply 1,200 feet in less than a mile to the 280 foot high cliffs on which the Mull of Kintyre lighthouse stood. A soft wind rippled the longer tufts of vegetation. Jane pointed out Rathlin Island and the Irish coast across the sun-dappled waters of the North Channel. The air was so clear that it was difficult to believe over twelve miles of sea lay between us and the blue land-masses on the horizon. I looked down to the lighthouse and saw where the conflicting tidal currents boiled the water even on this calm day.

It was very peaceful. I gazed past Jane's wind-stirred hair to the view of hills and ocean and distant mountains and thought how ephemeral human life is—not an original thought but none the less true for its triteness. A hundred years from now, both Jane and I would be gone but this July scene would still be here, new vegetation clothing the hills, the North Channel's waters still reflecting the sun. Unless man, with his skewed nature, managed to destroy his home. But I hoped that a hundred years from now the scene would still exist even if lighthouse and road were gone and that other men and women would enjoy it and sense the immanence of nature. I thought, not for the first time, that life was very strange. If I had not had that accident I wouldn't have met Jane—if she had been born a century ago (a tiny slice in the life of mankind) I could have come here, and not had the slightest knowledge that she had existed or might also have stood on this spot. I thought also that I was becoming uncommonly sentimental about a woman I had only met five days ago. Still, looking at that calm profile, I found I wasn't inclined to fight my feelings or to mock them.

After a few minutes of lazy comment we returned to the car. Travelling east again across the sheep-dotted moorland we descended almost to sea level at Carskiey. Jane glanced at me and slowed up as the car passed the wooded grounds of a large mansion house.

'That's the only place I know of where a ghost had a room of its own built specially for it. When the old mansion house—allegedly haunted by the wraith of a young girl who was murdered—was pulled down and reconstructed, a room was built in a turret with the old stones and fitted out with old furniture as a home for the little ghost so that it wouldn't wander through the rest of the house seeking familiar surroundings.'

I looked with interest at the house.

'I hope it's only a story,' I said, thinking of last night's seance.

Jane drove the car past the red corrugated barns of Lephenstrath Farm.

'What do you believe?' she asked.

I shrugged. 'I don't know. Some people get wild when I say I haven't sufficient data to come to a conclusion. "But you must have an opinion," they say. "Yes or no". They forget your opinion on a matter may be that you have no opinion.'

'I see. Yes. Very irritating to non-scientific types.'

'I know. I can only repeat what I said last night at dinner. I think the world is infinitely more complex than we can imagine. And it may be that the human animal's brain is just not capable of understanding it—any more than any of those sheep outside can ever appreciate our modern world-picture of planets, galaxies and expanding universe.'

'Surely that's a pretty dismal philosophy.'

'Not at all. Just a realistic one.'

We were now down by the shore, passing Keil Point.

'You see that mound to the left.' She pointed to a little hillock above an old graveyard. 'On top of it, cut into the rock, are St Columba's footprints. It's said he stood there and gazed across the water to Ireland and then, since he had taken a vow not to settle until he could no longer see his homeland, he journeyed on until he came to Iona.' She steered the Hillman Imp along the winding coast road.

'And the other side of the human coin. That headland about half a mile away is Dunaverty. There used to be a castle on that high isolated bit nearest the sea. In 1647 a covenanting army destroyed it, massacring every man, woman and child within its walls except, some say, one woman who escaped with an infant.'

I looked at the rock and thought of our own century's nightmares of gas chamber and nuclear hellfire.

We drove through the village, passed the coastguard station and the Argyll Arms Hotel. I lay back, perfectly content.

'Where are we going now?' I asked.

'Circular tour. Inland road to Campbeltown where you can buy me some afternoon tea, then back along the old coastal road to Southend. Very beautiful, very therapeutic.'

Her lips parted almost perkily and I wished I could see her eyes behind the dark glasses. I grinned in return.

'The tourist will stand the guide afternoon tea. Drive on!'

We passed Keprigan and the entrance to the Institute.

'This is where you had the accident?'

'Yes.'

The dark glasses swung in my direction.

'No nudgings of memory?'

'No.' I glanced out at the green banks whispering past. The terrified man's face appeared before the gate of memory and vanished again. I felt my forehead wrinkle.

'Don't worry, Alan. It'll probably come back. And even if it doesn't, I don't see that it matters. After all, most of the events of your past life have long gone beyond the recall of memory.'

I nodded. On impulse I told her about the terrified man. She shrugged.

'Impossible to say if it has any relevance. I shouldn't think so. Getting a bang on the head often shakes up old, long-forgotten memories, even childhood ones, quite fragmentary, their meanings lost long ago.'

'I'm sorry, Jane. I'm behaving like the typical hypochondriac who buttonholes the doctor at a party and describes his symptoms. I'm sorry. I won't do it again.'

'Nonsense. I asked you first.' She smiled. 'Feel free to describe your symptoms any time.'

I may take you up on that, I thought.

We had afternoon tea in the Argyll Hotel in Main Street—has anyone statistically-minded ever counted the number of Argyll Arms and Argyll Hotels in this part of the world?—then set off again. We had by now exchanged unsystematically a fair amount of biographical detail and I now knew among other things that she had been educated in Edinburgh, had studied medicine there, that both her parents were dead and that she had an elder brother something quite high up in the Inland Revenue.

The Hillman Imp was now on the Kilkerran Road, with Campbeltown Loch on our left. Jane, adopting her guise as guide again, indicated the tidal island of Davaar and mentioned its remarkable cave painting of the Crucifixion.

We now turned south on to the Learward Road and began climbing the steep hill away from the sea. This road, based on the old drove road that used to link Campbeltown and Southend, must be the most beautiful in the south of the Mull, in a number of places requiring really careful driving so that I was perfectly happy to be the passenger and be free to enjoy the sparkling blue sheet of the Kilbrannan Sound stretching out across thirty miles to the Ayrshire coast. It was a quiet road and the whine of the car as it climbed a steep gradient increased the loneliness. Very occasionally the silence was broken by the vicious metal rattle of a cattle grid as we passed over it.

I glanced at my watch. Four-thirty. There were still many hours of sunshine left. Oh, greedy Ramsay!

Jane pointed to her left. 'I've often wondered why they gave that hill the name of The Bastard,' she grinned.

'Perhaps someone tried to climb it.'

As we approached Benton Polliwilline, Jane said: 'It seems a pity to spend all the time in the car. There's a splendid beach at Macharioch. A cart track goes right down to the shore and it'll take the car so you won't have to walk more than a few yards.'

Some minutes more of slow descent among cultivated fields and we reached a large farmhouse. Jane guided the

Hillman Imp round past a gatehouse with a high broad cone-topped turret. The car began to bump over a low rutted track between a stone wall enclosing wooded grounds and a grassy bank. I noticed some standing stones —or possibly a ruined cairn—in a field on the slight rise between path and shore and resolved to mention them to John Marshall of the Cybernetics Department when I got back to Glasgow, his unlikely hobby being the study of megalithic remains.

Jane braked the car at the end of the track between sand-dunes. There were about half a dozen, white-painted caravans nested among the dunes like oversized gulls; on the sandy beach, two or three families sat while their children, brown in swimsuits, applied pail and spade or larked about in the bright water. We left the car. Jane pointed to a stone cross on a small, rocky headland about thirty yards away.

'There's another beach beyond that headland. Think you can make it?'

'Lead on.'

'I like humanity but on beaches I like to be by myself.'

'Born out of your station. Perhaps in a previous existence you were the lady of the manor here.'

She grinned. The point of the stick bit deeply into the sandy soil but the thatch of dune vegetation was easy on my ankle. The other beach we had to ourselves. On the grassy slope above it, I turned and tugged an imaginary forelock.

'Peasants all gone, Ma'am. All cleared away, Ma'am, by faithful retainer. Will Ma'am condescend to descend, Ma'am?'

'Ma'am will deign to.'

We sat down on the warm, powder-dry sand just below the grass-line. Two miles out Sanda Island and Sheep Island drowsed in the heat, sanctuaries for sea-birds. The sky was azure-blue and the silence was so complete it drew itself to our attention.

The rest of the afternoon slipped away like sand through a sandglass. For long stretches of time we were quiet, neither feeling the need to speak. When we did, it was usually to comment on sea or sky or the thin breeze that ruffled the tips of the coarse faded-green grass or to draw one another's attention to the behaviour of gulls or puffins. We did exchange a few more opinions and bits of information. I remember a moment when Jane was sitting, hands in lap, looking out across the water; lying, propped up on one elbow and turned towards her, I saw how the sun transmuted the downy hair on the nape of her neck to gold.

Quite suddenly, I knew we had reached that watershed in the non-static relationship between a man and a woman where both realise that the other's interest is more than casual, more than that due to mere social politeness; that from then on, it could develop, involving deeper, more vulnerable feelings, or retreat back into simple neutral friendship—or as neutral as it ever can be. On the other hand, I warned myself, it can often be a very one-sided involvement. I wondered what would happen if I kissed her. Yet although she was so desirable, so downright attractive, I found to my surprise that with this girl I had no intention at that moment of taking any step in that direction.

I looked down at my hand half-buried in the warm sand, raised it two inches and watched the jewelled sparkle of the grains cascading between my fingers. When I looked up again her face was turned towards me. Again the sunglasses effectively hid her eyes. Her warm mouth was slightly curved.

Oh God, I thought, if only women knew how our minds cycle: I want to kiss her and if she wants me to kiss her it'd be a pity if I didn't: on the other hand I don't want to spoil things because I'd hate to lose her—oh hell!

'When can I see you again?' I asked. Nothing, if not direct is old Rough-diamond Ramsay.

Her mouth curved a shade more.

'Yes, you must,' she said. 'After all, I've got to take those stitches out of your scalp.' The smile became impish. 'Perhaps we should be getting back now. Patient has been out long enough.'

We began the climb back over the headland. This time we approached the monument. It was about ten feet high, of red sandstone and shaped like a Celtic cross, standing on a large plinth. All four walls of the plinth bore inscriptions. Underneath a verse inscribed on the western side were the words:

'Lines written by the Duke of Argyll on a standing stone near this spot.'

I read the quatrain.

> 'Remember—this the only voice from thee,
> No other follows from thy sealed lips;
> With this thou greetest all the land and sea,
> With this thou hailest all the passing ships.'

Again, zephyr-like, an impression of our ephemeral nature touched me, so that as we moved away down the slope I halted and looked back. Jane regarded me curiously.

'Why do you do that?'

I shrugged. 'When a place I've visited has affected me or I've enjoyed myself there, I turn back when I'm leaving and get a last look—I suppose in case I never see it again.'

She shook her head in mockery.

'What a morbid fellow you are.' But I saw, with my heart leaping a little, that her smile was gentle and when I stretched out my hand she took it and made no effort to release it until we reached the car.

7 A splendour at midnight

I left Borgadel House on Monday after lunch. My head and my foot seemed back to normal apart from a few twinges from my ankle when I climbed stairs.

After breakfast Peter went off to the Institute and some two hours later Dorothy drove Mrs Davenport to Machrihanish Airport with, I suspected, a substantial cheque in her handbag. While she was away, I had coffee with old Mrs Campbell. I thanked her for her hospitality.

'We were glad to have you. I'm happy you have met Peter again.' Her remarkably sharp eyes twinkled. 'He told me you weren't impressed with Mrs Davenport.'

I chose my words carefully.

'Not convinced, Mrs Campbell.' I tried to warn her as gently as I could how extraordinarily complicated the whole business of spiritualism was, how even good mediums flourish for effect the information they have fished for, of the essential worthlessness as evidence of the phenomena we had witnessed. She heard me out patiently.

'I suppose you think that I'm a very foolish old woman, Alan'—I stirred, half-shaking my head—'but I cannot see that I am doing any harm in trying to contact my sons. I prefer to believe their spirits were here and that they will come again'—she hesitated—'and perhaps I may even see them next time. Mrs Davenport has agreed to come back next weekend.' There was nothing I could say so I took a sip of coffee. The old lady smiled. 'I know Margaret and Peter are not in favour of this but I intend to continue these sittings.' Her chin came up and I realised that there was yet another similarity to the Old Queen. 'I am hoping that I can persuade Alison to take part.'

I remembered Alison's chalk-white face and terrified sobs.

'I wouldn't advise that, Mrs Campbell. She isn't cut out for that sort of thing.'

She sighed. 'I haven't, in fact, much hope of persuading her.'

But there's a sort of moral blackmail, I thought, and that might work.

I had a chance to discuss matters with Alison herself when she drove me into Southend after lunch to collect my car. She seemed more rested though there were still smudges under her eyes. I asked her if she had got over Saturday's seance. Her knuckles whitened on the steering wheel.

'I'll never get over that.' We swung right at South Carrine. 'I'm sure somebody was in my mind. If anybody invites me to a seance again, I'll run a mile. As it is,' she almost whispered, 'I'll probably have nightmares about it for years.'

'Has Peter's grandmother spoken to you yet about sitting in again when Mrs Davenport returns next weekend?'

She flung me a startled glance. 'No. And I won't do it!'

'I think you're wise.' I hoped she would stick to her guns but I wondered just how much pressure sympathy aroused by the old lady's deep yearning would create. I resolved to have a word with Peter when I next saw him.

Alison waited on the main road opposite Muneroy's while I walked down the lane to collect my car. I was glad to find that using the clutch didn't hurt my ankle. Stopping just before Alison's car, I got out and transferred my hold-alls to the back seat of the MG 1100. Alison looked up at me, crinkling her eyes against the bright sunshine.

'Now don't overdo it.'

'I won't. I'll see you and Peter again soon.' I hesitated then smiled. 'I'm glad he's found you, Alison.' She smiled quickly in return.

I turned the car outside the white block of the Argyll Arms Hotel and followed the coast road westwards. Once inland, I continued north, passed South Carrine then took the left fork into Glen Breackerie. The road now became single track, with passing places. Across to the left, trees bordered the Breackerie Water. There were very few habitations—an old schoolhouse, the occasional farm. Anyone from the eighteenth or nineteenth centuries would have felt quite at home. Until, that is, the Glen narrowed near Low Glenadale and the Outstation appeared.

Behind the six foot high, wire mesh, perimeter fence, the station's late twentieth century hardware shared an area of 60,000 square yards with a gatehouse, two laboratories and the 'bunkhouse', the long barrack-room-like building used for admin, sleeping and eating. Beyond the United States Coast and Geodetic Survey Wild BC-4 camera on its concrete pier was the more recent Hewitt camera installation. Its big lens, thirty-six inches in diameter, with its fast f-ratio, enabled it to photograph satellites over one thousand times fainter than the dimmest star visible to the naked eye. And over to the right, the forty-five foot radio dish on its tower turned its girder-braced saucer to the sky, to collect information-laden signals from artificial moons or to listen to the whispers from radio objects sunk unimaginable distances away in space and time.

Surrounding the Outstation were the hills, mostly one thousand feet or more. Apart from the Mull of Kintyre's isolated situation and mild weather, the site at Low Glenadale had been chosen to utilise the hills' shielding effect so that optical and radio installations could operate at their maximum sensitivity. The work done to date had been principally of a site- and instrument-testing nature but in the next two years or so the Hewitt camera would begin its serious work as part of the Western Atlantic European Satellite Triangulation network and the USC and GS North Atlantic network, while the forty-five foot radio dish would be replaced by an eighty-five foot elliptical dish. At night, among the black bowl of the hills, with all station lights off and the stars glowing bright in their thousands, it was easy to imagine the solid Earth gone and the observer poised in a spaceship.

I had phoned Dr Black to let him know I would be returning to the fold that afternoon. Turning the car in at the gate, I passed the notice *Glasgow University Department of Geophysics Outstation* protruding from the flower-beds gloriously crowded with multi-hued Livingstone daisies and felt the events of the past five days recede in my mind. I put the MG in the tiny parking area before the bunkhouse and entered.

In the little office to the left of the entrance I found Croxley, the unlikely cultivator of the Livingstone daisies. An ex-naval chief petty officer, he did his best, with three assistants, to run the Outstation like a Royal Navy Shore Establishment. I suspected that our, to his eyes, undisciplined idle ways often made him wish he could give us a taste of navy drill.

Under his grizzled hair, his pale blue eyes glinted.

'Well, sir'—the 'sir' was transparently meaningless—'so you've managed to rejoin us.' Unspoken was the implication that I wasn't fit to be out on my own. He made a little note on a form. When I left the precincts I knew he or one of his minions would make another little note and eye me carefully just to see I hadn't the forty-five foot dish stuffed up my jumper. It was nothing personal of course. He did it for everyone, including the Director.

I nodded. 'Yes. Afraid I overstayed shore leave. Where's Dr Black?'

'In the computing room.' He paused. 'Mr von Neumann is using room two. Room three is made up for you.'

'Thanks.' I carried my holdalls down the corridor, left them in the little bedroom, not much larger than a British Rail sleeper, then retraced my steps and entered the big room in which much of the work required in tracking satellites was carried out.

Ten years after the launching of Sputnik I, there were hundreds of them in orbit, mostly American and Russian, but also a few British, French and others dipping their electronic toes gingerly in the shallows of space. By studying the way in which the spectral fingers of gravity twisted, elongated and tilted a satellite's orbit, as if it were a plasticine ring moulded by a giant, it was possible to measure very precisely the shape of the planet and obtain information about the deep interior. And by making observations of a satellite from places on the Earth's surface thousands of miles apart, their relative positions could be measured to an accuracy of a yard or two. Since most of the satellites we were interested in were also too faint to be seen with the naked eye, we required accurate predictions giving satellite positions on the sky background at various times. These predictions came to us from the World Data Centres but some time had to be spent modifying them for our purposes. Once we had taken a night's observations, the plates had to be processed and reduced. The results were then sent to the World Data Centres, helping them to prepare new predictions for us and several score of similar stations scattered across the five continents.

The work was engrossing and quite often at night, if I was not on duty, I used one of the smaller Moonwatch telescopes we had mounted on piers to fish for satellites. There was an eternal fascination about turning the 'scope to the predicted part of the sky, keeping an eye tight against the black rubber ring, maintaining a relaxed but vigilant watch on the slowly-drifting star field until suddenly a faint additional point of light would intrude at one side of the field and wander across the dim red lines of the graticule and you would realise that you had picked up a tiny man-made moon dropping through the silent skies.

I found Dr Black preparing the night's observing programme. We did have a scheduled list of objects chosen from the available predictions extending for as much as a month ahead but we usually left the final computations to the day before observing night. This seeming hand-to-mouth existence actually saved time since 'seeing' depended upon clear skies. If a patch of wet, cloudy weather set in, it rendered useless any predictions made for that period. We therefore depended a lot upon the meteorological service, which was highly accurate in its short-term predictions.

Dr Black looked up from the big chart table he was leaning over. On it were scattered mathematical instruments, prediction lists, charts with transparent overlays that converted orbital data into ranges, range-rates, altitudes and azimuths. At the table over by the window, von Neumann punched some figures into the Friden, watched the luminous display, wrote down the answer and nodded to me.

I apologised to Kurt for bringing him to the station especially when he was working on the final draft of his doctoral thesis.

'Oh that's all right. Are you fit again?'

'Yes.'

'Well, take it easy,' Dr Black advised. 'Concussion can have funny after-effects.'

'Oh, I feel fine. I'll help with tonight's predictions then take the afternoon off. Tomorrow morning after I return from the Institute it'll be business as usual and that'll let Kurt get back to the task of shovelling bones from one literary graveyard to another.'

'He is back to normal,' said Kurt, dryly.

About five-thirty, I completed the final position for Ariel III and added it to the list for the Hewitt camera operators. I refused the others' invitation to drive down to Southend after tea for a drink, explaining that I had a previous engagement. Jane had learned that I had never been to a ceilidh so when I asked her to let me see her again, she had suggested that we went to one being held in Port Mean on Monday night. The faint but unmistakable background of excitement I had felt all afternoon even while I calculated and measured and discussed priorities told me how deeply involved my feelings had become. When I halted the car in front of Jane's cottage near Carskiey later that evening, the sudden nervous dryness of my mouth emphasised the warning. I got out and opened the white gate.

Unlike one or two girls I had gone about with, she seemed to have some appreciation of time and was ready. Once in the car, she said:

'A Port Mean ceilidh is something no one who has ever

visited the Mull of Kintyre should miss. It's a relic, a survival from past centuries. I'm always scared television will spoil the inhabitants for this.'

'I'm looking forward to it. As long as you don't expect me to join in the Highland Fling.'

'Oh no. The first half of the proceedings is always a concert. Very little audience participation.'

We reached the junction and took the left fork, continuing down the twisting road to the Port. At eight-fifteen it was still daylight; this time, however, I was too busy guiding the car to study the neat, bright houses we passed between or appreciate the quicksilver glitter of the low sun reflected from the North Channel's waters.

'Go down to the harbour. The hall is across the green from the church.'

I followed her instructions. We parked the car and joined the people converging on the doorway of the hall like flotsam sucked into a sluice. Tickets, sold to us by a dark-tanned young fellow in faded blue shirt and jeans, cost two and sixpence each. He greeted Jane with a wide grin and a 'Hullo, Doctor, nice to see you'.

Once through a short wide corridor, we entered the main hall. The windows on either side were uncurtained, the close-packed rows of seats, mostly occupied already, were made up of an astonishing variety of kitchen chairs, benches, tip-up cinema seats, basket chairs—it seemed that almost anything that would accommodate a human bottom had been conscripted into service to line up raggedly on parade. The business end of the hall consisted of a broad foot-high platform flanked by closed doors to one side of which was a battered upright piano. Already the temperature was high and I reflected that if ten human beings' output of heat is equivalent to that of a kilowatt radiator, the hall would be blast furnace hot by the end of the evening.

'Any moment now,' said Jane solemnly, 'they'll produce the "sold out and sweaty" notice.'

The roar of conversation died as the master of ceremonies—'The local butcher' my companion hissed—took the stage and the show began.

It was genuinely enjoyable because of the complete friendliness of the audience towards the performers. The strains and tensions produced by the epidemic of rumours seemed to have been put aside for the evening. Many of the turns were of a very amateur standard; there was the inevitable accordion soloist, followed by the duet *The Crooked Bawbee*—the soprano was the bank manager's wife, the unstable baritone belonged to the chemist; there followed a comedian whose material was received with enthusiasm because the jokes were so blatantly old; there were recitations—an old kilted gentleman received TV studio audience applause for his rendering of *David and Goliath*, a young fiddler's nimble fingers spun strathspeys and reels, some of the tunes dating back to the salt water days of the Norsemen; there were a few kitchen comedy sketches—what did it matter if some of the artistes forgot their words and had to be prompted from the audience?—and before I knew it, it was 10 p.m. and time for tea.

I watched bemusedly while two men carried down the aisle a large grey zinc bathtub filled with cups whose extravagant variety and battered condition easily surpassed that of the seats. Tea-urns were next brought in; the cups were filled and passed along the rows from hand to hand, followed by sugar-bowls—use the spoon and pass it on—and quart-sized milk jugs. Two more men brought in large wooden bakers' boards bearing cakes and scones. Once these 'snasters' had been shovelled on to plates, they were distributed. Above the scone Jane bit into, I saw pure merriment glint in her eyes as she observed my reactions.

We were allowed ten minutes for tea before the MC called in the crockery and ordered us outside the hall so that it could be prepared for the next part of the evening's activities. Standing outside in the street, with the last light still tingeing the low cloud-bank in the western sky a pale pink, I welcomed the coolness of the night air.

From the open door of the hall, the sound of accordion and fiddle drew the dispersed audience back like the children of Hamelin Town. I saw that the seats had been placed backs against the walls; the plank floor had been swept clean of crumbs, cigarette ends and paper trash. The music was provided by three shirt-sleeved, perkily grinning fellows, their faces already shining with effort, the third plucking at a battered bass fiddle.

The dances followed hard on one another; Highland Schottische, Gay Gordons, Dashing White Sergeant, Strip the Willow. The dancers' enthusiasm was only a shade less than that of the musicians. Sitting out as I was forced to, I noticed that flasks and bottles of the 'water of life' circulated, more or less openly among some of the men, the fiddler in particular being refuelled so frequently that for most of the Eightsome Reel, he sawed away feverishly, a hard fixed grin on his streaming face, a glazed, unseeing film over his eyeballs until, the third time round, he staggered, swayed, was caught by two of his cronies, dragged out and his place and fiddle taken by another with a slickness that proclaimed it as standard operating procedure.

Jane had insisted that I be sensible and forgo dancing and had suggested that we wait only twenty minutes or so —in order to learn what the second half of a Port Mean ceilidh was like and to meet some of the inhabitants. She led me over to join a thin-faced man of about forty-five, wearing an open-necked shirt and clean but very old flannels. He had a stick by his side. He was tanned but gave an impression of frailty, even of transparency, enhanced by the sparse sandy hair and the pain-lines carved deep about his mouth. Yet his face was transformed by good humour and affection when he saw Jane and I immediately took to him.

'Korky, this is Alan Ramsay. Alan, Dugald McCorkindale.'

We shook hands. His grip was firm but his fingers seemed all bone. Jane sat down between us.

'Alan's spectating tonight. He ricked his ankle a few days ago.'

'I see. Takes his doctor about with him. Very wise.'

'This is Alan's first Port Mean ceilidh.'

'Ah!' Korky's mouth twitched. 'What do you think of it?'

'Enjoyable. I wouldn't have missed it for anything.' Which was quite true. The band finished the Gay Gordons and the MC encouraged us to form sets for the Dashing White Sergeant. The young fisherman who had sold us our tickets and a big fair-haired friend who could have been a descendant of a past Viking invader, and quite likely was, came confidently across to us and asked us to join their set. Jane looked undecided. I told her to go ahead, apologised to the pair for not participating and settled down to chat to Korky. Jane told me later that he had been smashed up in Korea, had a one hundred per cent disability pension and lived alone in a Port Mean cottage where he read a lot, talked with anyone on anything and thought deeply and tolerantly about our mixed-up human estate. He had also, it seemed, an interest in growing cacti, succulents and other plants. I thought of our burly ex-chief petty officer and his unlikely interest in Livingstone daisies.

Korky was completely free of self-pity and entertained me with his comments on a number of the dancers, downright to the point of saltiness, but not unkind. He was also completely direct in questioning me about my background.

Jane was returned by her partners, her face glowing. She seemed absurdly young, almost teenage in appearance and certainly giving no indication that she had gone through the long sobering training of a medical school. The next dance was announced and the blond fellow, with a perfunctory request to me for permission, asked Jane to dance.

'Go on,' I urged, feeling even more cloddish than before. To my dismay I found myself itchy with jealousy, wondering how often the fair-haired fellow had danced with Jane at past ceilidhs, whether I meant as little to her as I hoped he did, whether. . . . Oh, to hell! I jerked my gaze away from the dancers and found Korky's perceptive eyes watching me. He smiled.

'She's a fine girl, Alan. Absolutely no side and completely genuine. There's a lot of us in Port Mean have got very fond of her since she came here.'

He looked up and his expression changed abruptly, his mouth tightening in such obvious distaste coupled with a kind of baffled anger that I turned my head quickly. Three men approached us in a narrow vee. The man in the apex would have been tall if he had not slouched in slovenly insolence somehow matched by the greasy, unkempt shiny blue suit that hung on his neglected frame. His age was difficult to estimate; a blurred, brown wrinkled face with a red-veined whisky nose was topped with liquorice-strap hair. His eyes, grey pebbles, carried a jocose glint as if fortune, having unfairly deprived him of his rightful share of the world's goods, had finally poured the cornucopia over him. He was also drunk, enough to have a barely perceptible random walk about his gait but not enough to stone him completely. His companions were very much younger, possibly in their early twenties and obviously qualified for the loutish minority Jane had mentioned. They both had elaborate hairstyles, almost shoulder length; one, the brighter, subscribed to the jeans and leather jacket fashion school, the other, taller and broader, wore a frilly shirt and pants so tight he could have been waging a one-man crusade to bring back the codpiece. The two youths followed in the wake of the older man, they spectated, almost as if he somehow justified their existence and mode of life; they obviously approved of him, gloried in him while he in his turn encouraged them.

He stopped in front of us while the dancers moved like conflicting waves in the background and the music pounded out and surprisingly enough, his voice, though whisky husky, was clearly heard above the din.

'Well, Dugald, how are we tonight?'

'None the better of seeing you, Mackay.'

He gave a whinny of a laugh, echoed by his supporters.

'Now, now, Dugald, that's no way to talk to the elected representative of this community to the Argyll County Council. Is it, boys?'

I thought: he must be joking. But then a look at Korky's baffled face made me wonder.

'Aren't you going to introduce us to the doctor's friend, Dugald?'

Korky's face hardened. The smaller of the two youths sniggered.

'He wants to keep them to himself, Donald. Not very sociable, is he?'

He stuck his thumbs in the pockets of his jeans, pelvis out-thrust in parody of some pop-idol, his lips curled elaborately. Any moment now, I thought, and he'll do the cleaning-of-fingernails-with-knife bit. But I was wrong. His foot slipped.

'Oh sorry, Mr McCorkindale. Was that your stick? Sorry.'

He made no effort to retrieve it. I bent down, got it and returned it to its former position under Korky's chair. I felt a cold lump of angry tension grow in my stomach. Korky leaned back, his voice of cryogenic coldness.

'This is Donald Mackay, sometime scrap metal merchant, sometime garage hand, sometime licensed betting shop proprietor, now, God mend our insane minds, our elected representative to the Kintyre County Council. These two are Jamie Macdonald, potboy at the Anchor and Neil Parrish, apprentice joiner. They have not yet, for some reason, had electoral honours thrust upon them.'

The music and shouting stopped, a burst of clapping encouraged the players to give an encore and the dancing began again. In our corner we seemed unobserved.

While Korky spoke, Parrish's eyes moved from Korky's face to Mackay's, a broad grin revealing strong, nicotine-stained teeth. The grin had widened while his comrade had displaced Korky's stick and I replaced it. He now decided to escalate his side's baiting and to this end fished a cigarette packet from his pocket, lit one and leaned against the wall, back towards me, arm outstretched, his body angled away from the wall. He drew strongly at his cigarette, the end glowing cherry-red, used his free hand to take the cigarette from his mouth, blew a jet of smoke down on Korky's head and followed it with a half inch of ash before replacing the cigarette. I rose, contriving in so doing to hook his feet outwards. The jar of pain in my ankle was more than compensated for by the way Parrish's body hit the floor. From the frenzied rolling and scrabbling at his face, followed by a tender but blasphemous exploration of his nose, I deduced that the fire of his cigarette had been quenched in his left nostril.

'How clumsy of me,' I said.

He scrambled to his feet, lunged out towards me grab-handed and I sidestepped. Korky slipped his stick between his knees and for the second time he hit the floor. His momentum skidded him into the path of a trio, two sixteen stone women and a burly white-shirted and kilted bull of a man, backing away hand in hand and tippy-toed from their opposite numbers in the dance. I winced in sympathy as Parrish's last pint of air left his lungs as two of the trio landed on him. The kilted man rolled off Parrish, sat up, hands on floor and glared at the agonised youth, trying to draw some oxygen into his deflated chest. He got up, helped the stout, jumper and plaid-skirted lady to her feet before speaking in a soft, infinitely-threatening voice.

'So it's you, Parrish. I might have known. Sozzled again, no doubt.' Arms akimbo he glared at Macdonald. 'Aye and you too.' His fierce brown eyes under the grizzled crew-cut scanned our faces. 'Are these young idjits bothering you, Mr McCorkindale?'

Korky grinned, his hands resting on the now vertical stick. 'We were getting a bit tired of their company, Constable.'

'Right. Now get tae hell out of here the pair of you, or it's me that'll be having a wee talk with you.' With one meaty hand he dragged Parrish to his feet and practically slung his wheezing form at Macdonald and Mackay. One on either side, they supported their friend down the hall and out of the door. The constable watched them go, nodded to us then offered his arms to his partners.

'Let us get on with the dance now.' Which they did.

Korky looked at me.

'Are you always so clumsy?' he inquired mildly.

'Only when I'm nervous.'

'M'ph'm.' He drew a deep breath. 'They won't bother us again. They know that Constable MacCrimmon is liable to take them round behind the church and thump them and then run them in for breach of the peace.' His mouth twisted wryly. 'No. Parrish and Macdonald have simply been a bit above themselves since Mackay was elected county councillor. To them, empty-headed louts that they are, it's as if the bad man in a western town was elected sheriff.' He shook his head in perplexity. 'I said Mackay was a scrap metal merchant, worked in a garage, was a betting shop proprietor. The truth is he failed at all three, has voluntarily spent most of his adult life unemployed, is rarely sober and is mean and vicious into the bargain as his wife and family could testify. Up till the third week in May, no one in Port Mean had a good word to say about him. He was in fact the town ne'er-do-well. And then, just before the election, two members of our community propose and second him and he agrees to stand; although he makes no speeches and is drunk as usual most of the time and although he can be of no earthly use on the Argyll County Council, out of three hundred votes cast, he collects two hundred and four, the other three candidates, a banker, grocer and the hotel-owner's wife splitting the rest. It's unbelievable. But it happened. And now this specimen goes and represents us in Inveraray.'

I found the situation intriguing.

'But why? What do the others think about it?'

Korky ran his hand exasperatedly through his thin hair.

'I think they're mad,' he said simply. 'I asked some of those who voted for him. They had the most godawful reasons I've ever listened to—"I felt sorry for him", "I thought we needed a change", "I didn't like the others", "I thought responsibility would change him". The funny thing is, I had the most peculiar feeling they were astonished at their own answers. I really think the Port has gone sick in the past few months.' He saw me glance at the happy, hooching dancers, the spectators clapping in time to the music. 'I know. I look at them myself and I wonder if I'm the only one out of step. But there has to be something wrong with a community that elects a drunken wastrel like Mackay to represent its interests. And, as far as I can learn, now happily gives him extended credit in all the stores.' He paused, then added bleakly: 'And there have been other troubles too, in recent weeks.'

I remembered the minister's sermon. Korky bit his lip and the lines round his mouth deepened. 'When a situation like this occurs and there's no rhyme or reason in it you begin to wonder what is reality and what is illusion. There's a verse of George Campbell Hay's that's been running through my head lately:

' "The blin' shores o' Kilbrannan
in the mirky pit o' night,
they've watched the changin' colours
o' my port and starboard light,
they've heard my capstan drummin' round
in loch and kyle and bight."

'I just don't know which is port and starboard here.'

A long drawn out resounding chord signalled the end of the dance. The applause over, the dancers left the floor and Jane was returned to me. Sitting down between us she chatted with us during the next two dances and with several of the Port's inhabitants who came across to our corner. Finally we left. I shook hands with Korky, promising to visit his cottage the next time I was in the Port again.

Outside the building it was dark but clear, moonless but star bright. Below the harbour wall at the foot of the gently sloping green, the water placidly slapped at the stones. Behind us, muffled but still audible, the band struck up again, the thumps and shouts began once more. I helped Jane into her cardigan.

'How long will they go on for?'

'Two or three a.m. at least. Groups of them may even go back to houses for a sing-song and a supper-cum-breakfast.'

'Too late for me.'

'And me.'

I suggested that we walked to the end of the harbour before going back to the car.

'All right.'

We reached the harbour wall, picking our way over the rough, worn stonework and the tarry coils of rope.

'You didn't mind me leaving you with Korky so long?'

she asked. 'I didn't mean to, but it would have been stuffy to refuse to dance.'

'No, of course not.' My spirits rose absurdly. I felt the old longings, uncertainties, hopes take hold of me, the intense desire to know whether her feelings were involved as deeply as mine, the morbid fear that she wouldn't find in me anything to draw her to me.

At the end of the harbour we looked round. The hills were black flats, backdrops to the houses of the Port wrapped in darkness, except for one or two showing lights. From our position, the church eclipsed the hall where the ceilidh still continued unseen and unheard. The coal-black vault of heaven blazed with a myriad of coruscating diamond points of light, the abysses between the stars deepened by the glowing ice-cold band of the Milky Way tossed across the floor of the night. It was a sky you never see from a city, the sort of sky our ancestors must have gazed at in almost mindless awe. Understanding to some extent what I was looking at, I experienced once more that illusion of reversal of position, where I hung poised above the immensity, the solid Earth ephemeral behind me. I looked at Jane's raised profile. She spoke so quietly I could hardly hear her words.

'What's out there, Alan?'

'When I was a boy, my father used to tell me the stars were candlelights in distant cities. I always linked it with the nursery rhyme—what is it now?—something about a journey and candlelight.'

'How many miles to Babylon?
Three score and ten.
Shall we get there by candlelight?
Yes, and back again.'

I found myself smiling. Everybody was quoting poetry to me tonight. 'Yes, that's it. I'm afraid it's not so simple now. The sense of wonder is still there but the universe has taken on a new face. The distances, the numbers of worlds, are so large they're unimaginable. I find I think of the universe as a large and dusty hall. Choose one of the billions of floating dust-motes. That is our galaxy. Enlarge it to the size of the continent of Asia and the stars of the Galaxy are themselves dust specks, counted in their millions. One of them is the Sun with its family of planets in a disc the size of a penny. Enlarge that disc to the size of the same continent and somewhere in it is a ball fifty feet across. That is the Earth.' I grinned. 'End of lecture.'

I was conscious of her slim fingers in mine. She looked up again.

'And life? How many of these worlds have life on them?'

'Possibly millions of millions of millions.'

'How many intelligent species?'

'Anybody's guess.'

'Histories we know nothing of.' She looked at me. Beyond her head a solitary meteor crossed the sky to its incandescent destruction. The moment lengthened and I knew that its content, the splendour of the night sky, the faint breath of air about us, the dark sea and its whisper against the harbour wall, the pressure of her hand, our words, the meteor trail, would be woven forever into the fabric of my mind. I drew her to me, my left arm about her shoulders. She raised her head for my kiss. There was no boldness, no shyness, only the sweet, soft pressure of her lips on mine and the faint perfume of her hair.

When we drew apart, she regarded me quietly, her head slightly to one side. I leant forward, kissed her forehead this time and placed my arm about her shoulders again. Somehow I felt happy and sad at the same time.

'Let's go back to the car.'

Quite slowly we retraced our steps along the harbour wall. My mind sang, my heart pounded and the ever-present observer inside me marvelled at my emotional turmoil.

We drove back up the winding road out of Port Mean towards Carskiey. It was then she told me about Korky's history. When we reached her cottage I got out with her and opened the gate, faintly gleaming white in the darkness. I caught the fragrance of night-scented stock from the garden. Jane paused at the door.

'I've enjoyed the evening, Alan.'

'So have I.'

I put my arms around her and she allowed me to kiss her again. This time it was deeper, longer and I detected a quickening in her breathing when our lips drew apart. Her fingers stroked the side of my face, gently, then she drew back.

'It's late, Alan. I must go in.'

'I wish you didn't have to. I wish time could stand still . . .'

'Time waits for no man, etcetera, etcetera.'

'When can I see you again?'

'Quite soon.' She kissed me quickly. 'Phone me. At the Institute. Now, goodnight.'

' "Baby, it's cold outside." '

'Go. Outdated songs will get you nowhere.'

'What will, Jane, what will?'

She laughed. 'Time will tell. Goodnight.' She paused at the half-open door. 'And Alan.'

'Yes.'

'Drive carefully, my dear. I do want to see you again, very much, but not professionally. Goodnight.' The door closed and I paused, then slowly went down the path to the gate. I drove back to the Outstation, oblivious to everything but the knowledge that I was completely, hopelessly and irrevocably in love. Once in bed in my narrow room at Low Glenadale I lay, re-running the night's events. It was a long time before sleep came.

8 Portrait of a terrified man

I left the Outstation immediately after breakfast, assuring Dr Black that unless I was kept waiting at the Institute, I'd be back within the hour.

When I arrived at the Neurological Institute I left the MG beside three cars in a bay cut from the lawn area. Carrying the walking stick I had used, I climbed the steps in front of the glass door, smiling inwardly when I recalled the crabwise way I had gingerly sidled down them the previous Friday. Once inside, I crossed the polished hall to the reception desk and told the white-coated young woman what I was there for. She smiled.

'Just wait in the room across there.'

I did as I was told, after presenting her with the walking stick. I was not more than five minutes in the waiting-room before the taciturn, no-nonsense sister who had strapped up my ankle opened the door.

'Ah, Dr Ramsay. Please come with me.' We recrossed the hall. 'How do you feel now?'

'Very fit.'

We turned a corner into the tiled corridor and she opened a frosted glass door.

'Come in, please.'

The room had a desk with a chair behind it and a couch against the opposite wall. It resembled a doctor's consulting room with glass-fronted cases containing shelves holding shiny instruments; there were scales in a corner, of the lever type with a weight that slid along a slotted bar holding a weight pan. A photograph on the desk avoided scrutiny by brightly reflecting the sun's rays. A coat hanger hooked to a cupboard door carried a white coat.

'If you take a seat on the couch, Dr Ramsay, I'll get things ready.'

She disappeared through a doorway next to the window to return two minutes later with a tray bearing a kidney-shaped basin holding long surgical scissors in steaming water and a lemon-yellow aerosol spray. She now wore rubber gloves. Pushing the photograph to one side, she placed the tray on the desk and turned to stand over me. Out of the corner of my eye I saw starched apron and dark blue wrapper.

'Just tilt your head to one side.'

I did so. After a pause I felt and heard the scissors snipping at the knot of the first stitch followed by the tiny nip as it was snatched away. Two more came out. Then my eyes, fixed just a little tensely on the sunlit window, happened to turn in the photograph's direction, just beyond the glinting aluminium kidney basin.

It showed a group of people, obviously a staff photograph. Some of the men were in lounge suits, others in white medical coats; the nurses, male and female, were in uniform. I recognised Philip Ebor in the middle of the front row, seated; to his left and right were Dr Preston and Ramon. I couldn't see Jane. Another stitch was nipped out. Peter was there, smiling and happy. And then—my head jerked, a flood of memories bursting the dam.

'Keep still please. Did that hurt?'

'Sorry. No.' My eyes were locked on the face of a man in the back row.

'Just one more. There now.' Saliva in my mouth and the itchiness of sweat on my forehead and badly-scrambled pictures almost blotting out reality.

The clang of scissors into the basin, the hiss of the aerosol and the cool bite of the plastic dressing forming over the wound. *A man's terrified face.*

'There. Just keep it clean. Your hair will grow back in a few weeks.'

'Thank you.' I took a deep breath. 'Tell me, who is that man?'

'I beg your pardon?'

'In the photograph.' My outstretched finger trembled.

She hesitated, her face stiff with puzzled inquiry.

'That's a technician we had, a Mr Innes Carr.'

I managed to suppress my next question and substituted: 'Thought I knew him but it's a different name.' I paused. 'Is that all now?'

'Yes.' She picked up the tray. I rose.

'Thanks very much, Sister. Goodbye.'

'Goodbye. Take care of yourself.'

I left the room. In my bemused state I almost collided with O'Keefe. His eyes met mine.

'Hullo, back again, Alan?'

'Yes.'

His face took on a professional alertness. 'Are you all right?'

'Yes. Just got the stitches out.'

'Oh, I see. Not a major operation.' He must have read something of my inner turmoil for he added: 'What's wrong?'

'Have you a few minutes to spare?'

'Certainly. What is it?'

'I've recovered the memories I lost. In there, while I was getting the stitches out.'

His face registered puzzlement.

'You mean they just came back like that?' He snapped his fingers.

'Yes.'

'Sometimes happens that way.' He frowned, concern on his tanned features. 'But you seem a bit . . . shaken?'

'Yes, I am. These memories—they're a bit disturbing.'

He took my arm.

'Look, come along to my room and tell me about them. That is, if you'd care to.'

'I'd like to. You're sure I'm not keeping you away from something important?'

His white teeth flashed. 'Nothing that can't wait. Come along now.'

We turned and walked along the corridor, climbed a flight of stairs to the second storey and came to a door with his nameplate on it. He unlocked it and ushered me in. It was a large airy room with comfortable modern furniture, sectional bookcases well-filled with hard-covers and paperbacks, the walls carrying bright impressionistic paintings in which orange and lemon hues contrasted successfully with purple shadows. Without being able to point to anything in particular being responsible, one got the impression that something of the sunlight and colour of the Caribbean had been cleverly integrated into the decor.

He crossed to a well-stocked drinks cabinet.

'I know it's early,' he said, while he poured, 'but I prescribe a medicinal whisky.'

He ushered me into an armchair on one side of the artificial log fire and took a seat opposite me, his glass amber in the sunlight.

'Well, now. What disturbed you about your recovered memories?'

I told him about the image of the terrified man who had disturbed my sleep on a number of occasions. He nodded but said nothing.

'I now know who he is.'

His head tilted.

'There was a photograph on the desk of the room where I got the stitches out. It was a staff picture. You're in it . . .'

'Ah yes. Taken a year ago just after I came. I know the one.'

'One of the technicians, a fellow called Carr. He's the man I keep seeing.'

Ramon's eyes registered scepticism though he schooled his features to neutrality.

'Are you sure? Are you sure you didn't seize on a superficial resemblance to give a name to your bogeyman —you know: name a fear and it loses its power.'

I found myself shaking my head emphatically.

'No. No! It is him.'

O'Keefe markedly steered away from the point.

'But what about these memories of yours? I assume

they are of the events just prior to the crash.'

'Yes. You'll see in a moment why I'm so sure.' I fixed my gaze on a painting that evoked the idea of lush tropical vegetation while my visual memory re-ran the last few minutes before I lost consciousness. My car had been on the inland Campbeltown–Southend road. I'd got on to the straight part just past the Brecklate road junction. I wasn't travelling fast, the day was pleasant and I was enjoying the drive. Then, just at the point where the Conieglen Water meets the burn from Glen Kerran I sat up, tense, feet slamming down on clutch and brake. A few yards ahead of the car, a man had scrambled through the hedge on the left-hand side of the road, oblivious to the scratches it must have cost him, stumbled on the road, sagged to one knee, his hand starfish flat on the tarmacadam, recovered himself, turned desperately towards the approaching car and ran to meet it, hands upraised as if seeking death under its wheels, his terrified face streaming with sweat, eyes staring, beseeching. The shrieking car slid to a halt no more than two yards from him, the bonnet slewed round into the hedge. I relaxed my anguished grip of the wheel, shock-released adrenalin pouring through me, imprinting indelibly the man's appearance, and flung open the door even as a second man crashed through the hedge behind the first. I scrambled out, straightened up, the clatter of the running man's feet on the road urgent in my ears then the world exploded in a blinding light that faded like a dying flare while the fields and sky wheeled and the warm bonnet came up and bludgeoned my face and all sensation ceased.

I stopped speaking. Ramon had listened without interruption.

'And after that?'

'I woke up here in the Institute.'

He rubbed his jaw, his eyes troubled.

'And the first man?'

'Carr, the technician in the photograph.'

'I see.'

'Peter mentioned a technician who left suddenly.'

Ramon grimaced. 'But look here, Alan. You're implying

that your car accident is much more complicated than you thought.'

'Where is that technician? Did you ever learn what happened to him?'

He shook his head. To avoid replying he placed his empty glass on the small occasional table beside his chair. A shimmering blue circle of light expanded out from it and I blinked. The ring burst into motes when it touched me, like jewelled water globules in free space. I found myself concentrating very hard on the table lamp beside the glass. The pale nude figure of the woman, her outstretched hands supporting the large parchment cylinder, was slowly melting, flowing, bending as if viewed under the sea-green waves of ocean. I concentrated, warmth cocooning my body. I heard Ramon's voice. Somehow his normally pleasant tones had a burbling, tweeting, electronic component in them.

'He came back, like all satellites in orbit, plunging round the world'—vision of a green and blue and white globe spinning—'like beads on hoops.'

A child's abacus, mine, but its red and black glistening beads are on interlocking rings; its significance is overwhelming, crushing, if only I could interpret it. I touch the rings and they spin, plangent, *glissando* tones harmonic and soothing.

The words cease, rings of many colours emerge from his mouth like smoke, ellipses distorting themselves in perspective like Lissajous figures. The impressionistic painting was ablaze now—*nec tamen consumebatur*—its raw orange hue hurtful to the eye and screaming like a klaxon horn, the deep purple background suddenly present only as the cut-out absence of orange while the ebony frame began to expand or I began to shrink and Ramon's body was giant-like looming over me like a colossus—of Rhodes, a Rhodes scholar. I raised my hand and sudden mind-cringing terror enveloped me as I saw how brittle, crystal-like my fingers had become, how they shattered even as I watched, the shards tinkling outwards like the artificial snowflakes in the glass snowstorm I now inhabited. The nails, tiny lozenges of pink, except where the half-moon cuticle gleamed, hovered in rows before me, windows in a railway carriage, each containing a tiny face, each different, each little mouth writhing in silent conversation. Then the whole scene tore like a sheet of damp Kleenex, the black abyss between the fragments widening as I lost my grip on the world and I felt consciousness float and melt like snow fallen into a winter stream's dark waters, a moment there then gone forever, forever, forever . . . forever. . . .

Book two   Allegro con fuoco

9 Second awakening

Blackness. Blackness shot with red. Warmth. Consciousness scattered like a child's toys at the end of day. Eyelids open. My eyelids. Mouth dry. I am . . . Peter Campbell. I am in bed. Cool, crisp linen tight about me.

Where am I? I have run a long way and seen many places and now I am home. Not home. No. But I know what I mean. The ceiling is blue. Silence. I turn my head. There's a white plastic-topped bedside locker, nothing on it. I raise my head. Slight ache, nothing much. There's a chair beside the bed. The room is small and narrow—there's no window. Odd. A cream-hued fitted wardrobe. I recognise nothing. And yet . . .

Now I notice above the bed a panel with switches and a push-button. I've been ill? I sit up. I don't feel weak. The slight ache is worse. Thoughts, conflicting, antagonistic, spill on to my mental stage, turning it into a battleground. I close my eyes tightly, clenching my teeth, clutching the red top blanket into great folds to avoid extinction, submergence in the flood of images.

I am Peter Campbell: hold on to that. Vision of car crashing, scream of metal, tyres—someone with me—no safety belt on—through windscreen, shattering into pale sugar tablet fragments. Who is it? WHO IS IT? Images oscillate in and out of focus, leapfrog past each other, the hospital room almost blotted out behind them. Car crash, white-coated men, Borgadel House, Keprigan Road with its green borders and quiet, watching hills. A study, brown furniture, a desk with a dark-suited, tireless figure behind it, listening, talking, writing. X-ray theatre—operating theatre? Ceilidh, dancers, a scuffle, a girl comes towards me—Alison? No! Alison is dead. A long time ago. A nursery rhyme—how many miles to Babylon? An empty, unbearable aching constricting my chest. An office; paperwork, the daily routine. A large comfortable sitting-room and my grandmother's plump, placid face saying, 'Yes, take Alison with you by all means. But be back before dinner. I'm expecting Mrs Davenport.' Alison screaming; darkness and a wire mesh fence and large spidery installations black against the jewelled field of night. A dining hall, two dining halls flickering in and out of each other like quick dissolves on TV; my mother's face, eyes disapproving—you can do so much better, Peter, remember your position, Peter. A stone cross—remember—this the only voice from thee, no other follows from thy sealed lips—steady, hazel eyes, merriment, affection, sweetness—I am . . . Alan Ramsay.

Sudden exploding pain and a quick gasping, audible scramble from beckoning illusion back to reality—No! No! Peter Campbell. I am Peter Campbell. Don't fall back now. Peter Campbell. Not . . . Alan Ramsay. More pain. Unbearable so that I scramble out of bed and am standing barefoot on the floor when the door opens.

The white-coated man framed there had a slab-like, watchful face. His broad shoulders tightened the coat across his chest, his hands hung by his sides, capable, weighty implements. 'Good afternoon, Mr Campbell. You're awake now. How do you feel?'

My mouth opened but no words came. The man—attendant, my mind shouted—approached.

'You're probably very thirsty.' *A locker and a glass jug of water and a nurse helping me to drink.* The man crossed to the wardrobe door, opened it, the catch clicking and I glimpsed a suit of clothes on a coat-hanger; beside the suit hung a grey dressing-gown with scarlet piping. The man helped me into the dressing-gown. Quite automatically I tightened the cord and fastened it. The twisting fibres of the cord and the thistle-shaped tassels were silky-smooth to the touch. He handed me a pair of brick-red slippers which I slid my feet into. 'Now then, if you come with me I'll take you to Dr Ebor.'

He took my arm in a helpful grasp that I somehow knew could become vice-like and I found myself walking out of the room like an automaton. There was a slight feeling of weakness, a minor unsteadiness of the legs as if I had been days in bed. All this time the tide-race, the tumbling, conflicting spate of images maelstromed through my brain. The 'I' of personality was a poor, harried turncoat who changed his allegiance every second under the unceasing onslaught of pictures and voices.

The corridor was dull, even in electric light, its walls oak-panelled to chest height, the floor carpeted brown. It was not long in the direction in which I was being guided and at the end I could see a large window through which wooded grounds were visible. We seemed to be on the ground floor. For a moment the dimly-seen trees and dark, brooding exterior suggested late evening and then I recalled with fleeting unease that my companion had implied that it was afternoon. We approached a door labelled 'Dr Philip Ebor' and my companion knocked. A voice invited us to enter.

Again electric light. The large room was familiar as was the man seated behind the long desk. He wore a dark grey suit; a white coat hung up on a brown door to the right of the curtain-edged window—*a white coat hung up, a clang of scissors in a bowl, a . . .*—through which another view of the gloomy grounds was visible. I got an impression of two brown-leather, cushioned armchairs before the desk, a long couch against the wall to the left, a tray of drinks including several tumblers and a large glass jug of orange juice—my mouth blazed with thirst—a glass-fronted bookcase weighty with volumes, and several seascapes on the walls, soothing, palely luminous. On the wall above the fireplace, in which a coal fire burned pleasantly, a sunburst clock registered four thirty-five. The conflict between the time and the evening light outside scraped at me anew.

Philip Ebor stood up, a smile on his strong features. He

came round the end of the desk.

'Ah, Peter, so you've come out of it. Come and sit down here.' He indicated the nearer of the armchairs. I sat down, leaning back, arms on the leather supports. 'George, get Mr Campbell a glass of orange juice. He'll be as dry as the Sahara. In fact, bring me a glass too, please.'

He returned to his seat behind the desk. It held the usual furniture, a calendar, a communicator, a telephone, a desk pad, a large white blotter with a buff file on it and a pen and pencil holder. I accepted the glass of thick orange juice, freshly squeezed, and drank half of it. The smooth cool liquid was exquisite in its thirst-slaking action. Ebor sipped his before placing the glass on the blotter.

'Thanks, George. You can leave us now to have a talk.'

'All right, Doctor.'

I heard the door close gently behind me. Ebor indicated the door his white coat hung against.

'You don't want to . . .?'

'No . . . thanks.' I knew, somehow, that behind that door was a small toilet and washroom. Ebor's grey eyes examined my face.

'Well, Peter, how do you feel?'

'Look, I'm utterly confused. I . . .' I broke off, my mind gyrating wildly.

'I'm not surprised. We've had to give you one hell of a jolt.' He paused, regarding me narrowly, as if apprehensive, at least as much as Philip Ebor ever could be.

'You do know who I am?'

'Yes. Philip Ebor.'

His almost Amerindian face relaxed.

'Good. And George?'

'George?'

'You don't recognise him?'

'No.' I paused then asked hesitantly: 'Should I?'

He avoided my eyes. 'You should, but that's not terribly important. What is important is how you are.' It was his turn to pause. 'Who are you?'

His voice was deep, resonant, interrogatory.

'Peter Campbell' and 'Alan Ramsay' sprang out of my subconscious like two horses when the starter's gate leaps up; pain, attendant images like a movie film cut into fragments, scrambled, rejoined and speeded up, wrenched at my mind. I stammered.

'I—Peter Ca—no! Alan—I.' I found I was panting like a dog, sweat pouring down my face.

'Take it easy,' he said quietly, concern on his face.

I licked the salt from my lips, forced myself to drink some more orange juice. My teeth chattered on the glass. *Teeth chattering and a girl screaming in terror.*

'Do you remember our last talk?' he asked.

Again the eerie duality of thought, of observing two cinema screens at once. *The dining-hall at the Institute, Ebor, Ramon, Peter—I am Alan!—Jane, dear God, Jane! —this room, this seat, Ebor: 'I think we'll try something else, Peter: it's drastic but it might break you loose.' I'm listening, the rooms, the words are being stored in memory even while I'm in another world, living my life as Alan. It won't work, Ebor; I don't want to return to the world where she's no longer alive . . .*

I felt my head swaying.

'I've two—I seem to have two memories of two last talks.' I tried to explain, faltered miserably and he nodded. He seemed pleased.

'So we *were* reaching you. Some part of you was listening.' He laid his own glass down beside the telephone and softly at first, then more and more strongly, while an infinitely sly, self-congratulatory wave of suspicion flooded over me, a new thought train arose to dominate my brain. Why place his glass there? Exactly two point three inches to the left of the telephone. It's a signal. He has someone watching. He's planning some evil with them. Against me. There! He's leant back now. What does *that* move mean? One part of me watched in fascinated horror the paranoic logic develop, seizing me mentally by the throat. Then, quite suddenly, the insane mood exploded like a toy balloon and I could hear Ebor again, could sit in misery while he talked.

'. . . it seemed reasonable to me, though I'm afraid Dr Preston had other opinions. I felt that although you appeared to be living entirely encapsulated within your construct, there had to be some part of you paying attention to reality, simply because you were still able to feed yourself and walk about.' The muscles of his cheeks hardened momentarily. 'You hadn't withdrawn yet to the stage of complete catatonia, of having to be fed, etcetera.' I listened, frozen, refusing to accept the implications. 'So I felt that you might still be jolted, at least part of the way, back to reality. If this succeeded, you might then be able to face your problem and solve it . . .'

A knock at the door made him break off. 'Come in.'

I sat facing him, my mind screaming its desire to flee from the grotesque picture he was painting of my mental condition, my brain only half-attending to the woman's voice behind me.

'Oh, I'm sorry, Doctor, I didn't know you had anyone with you. It's Mr McCorkindale. Another attack. A bad one this time.'

Ebor bit his lip. 'All right, I'll come at once, Sister West.'

Quite distinctly I felt the small hairs at the nape of my neck bristle. Reluctantly I turned my head. In blue wrapper, white apron and cap, Dorothy West stood in the open doorway. I felt my mind cringe like a snail retreating into its shell as I realised that the smile she gave me was one of common politeness, the customary staff-meeting-patients smile.

As Ebor strode past me he said: 'Look, Peter, I'm sorry but this seems urgent. Would you go back . . . No. Just remain here quietly till I return. It's more comfortable. Then we can finish our talk. I won't be long.'

I remained staring bleakly at the door after it had closed behind him and Dorothy.

A wall of unbearable pressure forced me to my feet and I crossed to the window. It was dimmer now outside, only trees and bushes being visible through my dark reflection. My eyes sought the clock face. Four forty-five. I seized the handle of the door to the right of the window, turned it and pushed inwards. The small cupboard-like side-room contained a gleaming wash-hand basin against the left wall with a mirror above it. Facing me was a toilet. I hesitated, trying to soak up the dregs of my courage. Then I stepped forward and faced the mirror.

A wave of despair, black, crushingly depressing, engulfed me even as it seemed that all life poured from my sagging body. My hands gripped the cold vitreous enamel of the basin edge. The face that stared back at me above the reflection of pyjamas and grey dressing-gown was roundish, smooth, anxious. It was Peter's face—mine.

With a sob I whirled back into Ebor's room. I found my eyes on the desk calendar. It was one of the universal ones with slots for day, number and month. The black letters and numbers on their ivory slots danced against the maroon surround.

Thursday
10
January

With trembling fingers I picked up the calendar and stared at it in an irrational hope that by will I could alter it. That couldn't be the date. Ebor or his secretary couldn't have changed it for months. But a part of me sniggered wryly at the hollowness of the reasoning and recognised how well the date solved the problem of time of day and the semi-darkness outside, the lighting conditions of midwinter. I leaned forward, my right hand flat on Ebor's desk, my left gripping the slightly protruding edge, for what seemed aeons until the typed name on the white label of the buff folder registered in my dulled mind.

Peter Campbell

I dropped into Ebor's chair, opened the folder and began to read the typed lines, sometimes scanning a paragraph at almost feverish speed, at other times finding my attention arrested while my mind acknowledged and assessed and a hopeless bitterness spread within me like spilled coffee over a tablecloth.

'Present state of patient report: collated and summarised from case-notes filed under C14.

Dictated by Philip Ebor, January 4.

'Peter Campbell had been employed by the David Campbell Neurological Institute as business administrator for fourteen months when he had his car accident. As Director I therefore was often with him and the conversations I had with him together with the opportunities I had of observing the family on the occasions I visited Borgadel House socially, gave me considerable knowledge of the inter-family relationships and stresses there and enabled me to understand relatively quickly the nature and causes of his illness.

'Throughout the first twenty years of his life, Peter was completely dominated by his mother, his father, although highly intelligent, a successful neurosurgeon and fond of his son, being almost a non-personality in the home circle. His mother's bigoted, irrational views on religion, sex, social status, in fact all the major factors that drive human beings, were continually forced upon Peter. Even in his late twenties, when he would appear to most people to have thrown off her cramping, distorted world picture, I have no doubt they still possessed considerable charge within him, crippling his ego and hamstringing his dealings with the world.

'It is, I think, significant that he has had many girl friends but married none of them, the early episodes being terminated by his mother's actions. But while he was at Borgadel House and employed here, he fell deeply in love with his grandmother's secretary, Alison Cadell. She returned his love. She was, in fact, the sort of affectionate, uncomplicated girl who would have made Peter a satisfactory wife and would have brought him a greater measure of security and perhaps have matured him. His mother, of course, opposed the marriage; his grandmother approved.

'After a quarrel with his mother concerning his engagement, Peter drove away from Borgadel House in a rage. Alison was with him, in the front passenger seat. As often happens, his anger affected his driving. He turned a corner at too great a speed, saw a farm lorry backing out of a field, tried to brake and Alison, who unfortunately was not wearing a seat belt, was catapulted through the windscreen, hit the side of the lorry and was killed instantly.

'Peter's injuries consisted of a few bruises on the side, some cuts and concussion. The accident occurred near Keprigan on July 27th and he was brought here. He has been here ever since.

'Peter made a rapid recovery from his physical injuries but has been totally unable to face the fact that he has lost Alison, not only killing her by his careless driving but by careless driving brought about by his quarrel with his mother. Her actions, though unintended to have this end-effect, have once again removed a girl from his life.

'He was unconscious for two days. He showed great distress when told of Alison's death, to such an extent that he had to be sedated. When he was allowed out of bed three days later, his protective psychosis was already well-formed, his statements and behaviour making it quite clear that it would have been unwise to let him go. By the middle of August his retreat into the world he had constructed was well-nigh complete and he could be reached only by using hypnosis. In a number of sessions over the rest of August and the first half of September, it was possible to learn how skilfully he had elaborated his first crude attempt at protecting himself from reality by a simple denial of the facts.

'In his student days he shared lodgings with a science student Alan Ramsay. Ramsay's parents were dead, having been killed—significantly?—in a road accident; his aunt put him through university. In Peter's eyes, Ramsay was therefore in the enviable state of not being under parental influence, was independent and free from the guilt feelings, moods of rebellion, the uncertainties Peter experienced.

'And so after the car accident Peter "became" Alan Ramsay. He had gone—escaped?—to America, worked there for a number of years and was now back in Scotland. Peter remembered that Ramsay had entered space research—again, an escape from this world, from Mother Earth?—and to use his knowledge of the Mull of Kintyre he had Ramsay come over to the Mull to work in a space research station at Low Glenadale. We have in fact checked this out. It is all true except that the real Ramsay is still with NASA at Goddard Space Flight Center. The information about Peter's student days supplied by the real Ramsay in a letter he sent us in reply to our inquiries has helped to illuminate Peter's relationship with his mother. Interviews with his mother have not been of much direct help.

'With an economy that still fascinates me, Peter has used real events to fill in the details of his dream world, re-arranging them like a man who demolishes a house then builds one of entirely different style from the fragments. As Alan, he has a car accident—a minor one, however—that necessitates his recovery in the Institute. There he meets Peter, a happy, useful Peter in a world Alison Cadell still lives in, with sunshine every day since it is still the height of summer. Alan visits Borgadel House, sees how happy Peter is with Alison, how helpless his mother is to prevent their marriage. Sister West, on our staff, is transformed into Dorothy West, housekeeper to Peter's parents and used in the age-old sexual phantasy of the complaisant, older, but attractive experienced woman who initiates the young man into the art of love, thus, in the present case, enabling Peter to score off his mother. Note: there may well be an echo of the Oedipus complex here since Sister West and Margaret Campbell are not dissimilar in appearance.

'And finally, the tender emotions, the feelings Peter still has for Alison are utilised in his assumption of the "Alan" personality by creating a girl specially for him—not just any girl but a young and attractive member of the staff here, a Dr Jane Selkirk, whom he encounters when he, that is, Alan, is recovering from his accident. After he is discharged, they go out together, for example to a Port Mean ceilidh (to which Peter went with Alison so that the mental props are ready for use), they fall in love.

'Unlike most of the characters in his fantasy, Jane Selkirk seems to have no basis in reality, there being no member of staff of that name or description, nor can we find anyone resembling her in his past life. She would appear to be completely fictitious; perhaps she is the projected image of the ideal woman all men carry within themselves.'

. . . The blue sea reflecting the sun and a soft wind stirring a girl's dark hair and a moment in eternity, a gentle

smile, the touch of a hand . . . the splendour of the starlit night and the whisper of water against a harbour wall and . . .

Tears stung my eyes, blurring the typescript and my throat burned raw. I closed my eyes tightly then opened them and forced myself to read the little that remained.

'Yet there would appear to be elements in this unreal world that indicate an attempt by some mechanism in Peter to force him to an awareness that behind his pleasant world, there lurks a different reality. He has heard Alison screaming; he blocks this by manufacturing a seance in which she is entranced and "taken over" and screams. He is bothered just before "sleep" in his world by the vision of a terrified man (himself); he constructs a man who caused the accident—again an admission that he is responsible? —by darting out in front of his car. But the man is quickly given an identity from a staff photograph he has seen so many times, that of a technician who resigned and left six months ago, and an explanation is concocted, nebulous and still disturbing but no longer a threat to his world. And so on.

'Peter now resents and hates anyone who attempts to break into his illusion. We have tried without success every orthodox method including hypnosis, shock treatment, both by insulin and by electricity, prolonged sedation and a recent attempt to disturb the closed cycle electrical currents sustaining his fixation by implanting microelectrodes in his brain. This last attempt, necessitating a quite small operational wound, was also a failure; indeed Peter has subsequently incorporated the wound into his phantasy as a gash received when his car crashed. We now intend to use a combination of methedrine and lysergic acid diethylamine in the hope that during the forty-eight hour period he is under its influence, his brain mechanisms will be able to separate illusion from reality.

'If we fail, the prognosis is bleak. A deeper retreat into his dream world where Alison still lives and the sun always shines because it is always summer; with complete severance from the real world, outwardly manifested by total catatonia until death finally releases him.'

10 The mirky pit o' night

My head ached and a cold weight of depression crushed me as if the room lay at the bottom of the deepest ocean of Earth and tons to the square inch of pressure squeezed me on every side. With chilled fingers I closed the buff folder, my mind still struggling to free itself from the welter of conflicting memories and impose some sort of order on the world. Which world? Which personality? I held my bowed head, elbows on the desk. If only I could think straight. I am Alan Ra . . . Pain lashed at me. No. I am Peter Campbell and Alison is dead. Face it! But I felt my grip on reality slacken and I knew I had to do something before Alan Ramsay forced out Peter Campbell again and the soft, sunny illusion enveloped me once more, painting out the harsh winter world of disaster. I pushed the chair back, got up and moved to the window. I had my back towards the door when it opened and Ebor entered.

I turned to face him. He looked tired but put on a smile.

'Sorry about that, Peter.' He sat down behind his desk and leaned back.

'Well, how do you feel now?'

The momentary clear spell was past, the short episode of decisive thought was over, the clattering, buffeting impressions had me again. I stood, shoulders bowed as if under a physical battering.

'I am Alan Ramsay,' I ground out while a despairing part of me screamed: 'No, Peter Campbell, Peter Campbell, not Alan Ramsay!' I wrenched my head from side to side, almost sobbing under the internal conflict.

'I—don't—know. I . . .' I broke off.

Ebor rose to his feet. His voice held encouragement and hope and compassion.

'Don't give up, Peter. You've come back a long way. Four days ago we couldn't have talked like this. You were inaccessible. Now, after one treatment, you've partially broken through. I think we're on the right lines at last. To-morrow, we'll continue the treatment. In the meantime, I suggest you rest in your room. You'll have a light meal and a sedative and in the morning we'll have a further talk before proceeding with the course.'

He must have pressed a bell-push for the door opened and George entered.

'Take Mr Campbell back to his room now, George.'

A wave of exhaustion swept over me. I walked almost somnambulantly along the corridor, George holding my arm at the elbow. Back in my room, George grinned.

'All right, dreamboy, off with the dressing-gown.'

Resentment flared weakly within me at the unconcealed derision on his face but it seemed too much of an effort to protest. I sank on to the edge of the bed and watched him hang the dressing-gown in the wardrobe. When he'd left, I sat, hunched up, a part of my mind wondering dully why he inspired such fear, another part hammered anew by the competing Campbell-Ramsay personalities.

I must get out of here, I told myself, feeling my body shudder as a fresh nervous spasm seized it. I moved to the door. The relief when I found it to be unlocked was numbing. A fugitive thought—of course nowadays they've done away with locks and bars—shuttled bleakly through my head as I peered into the corridor. There was no one about. I took the suit from the wardrobe, throwing it on to the bed, found a shirt, pants, socks and black shoes in the drawer underneath, and dressed feverishly, my fingers trembling, my attention strained to detect any sound of approaching footsteps.

When I left the room, I made for the large window at the end of the corridor, unsnibbed it and hauled on the brass handles. It was stiff but not beyond my strength.

Light from the corridor splashed off trees and bushes and, directly ahead of me some forty yards away, a wall. I straddled the sill, jumped down, pulled the window shut behind me. Stepping aside out of the beam, I followed it to the wall.

I reached up, my hands sought a grip on the rough cool broad coping, my raised left foot found a slight toe-hold in the wall and I heaved myself to the top, to lie full-length upon it. As far as I could see in the almost total darkness beyond, there was a track of sorts separated from the wall by a grassy bank. A hedge bordered the other side of the track; fields, smudgy, too dim to be seen clearly, rose to a dark, hilly horizon. To the left the track entered a wood; to the right it disappeared round the corner of the wall. As far as I knew I had never seen it before.

I dropped down, slid down the bank and stood uncertainly on the path. Left or right or through the hedge. Left, into the wood. Like a wounded and hunted animal I wanted to conceal myself. At a jog-trot, my feet thudding softly on the beaten earth of the track, I started off, my mind bruised, my thoughts garish and tattered, fear and despair driving me on. The deeper, cathedral darkness among the trees enveloped me, their tall trunks pencilled blackly on all sides, their upper foliage merging so that only directly overhead as at the end of a tunnel could the grey sky be seen in patches. Once or twice a star crossed a patch of sky.

The track was climbing now and twisting. I ran on, stumbling at times over a tree root, always recovering and hastening onwards as if I could leave behind the raw emotions and millrace of images within me. At times I was Alan Ramsay—'I am Alan Ramsay; this is a nightmare, I'll waken, it's a dream, I must waken'; at others my mind insisted I was Peter Campbell, fighting desperately to survive, to keep hold on reality, to retain some sort of sanity for just a few minutes more.

The trees were thinning now. I seemed to be reaching the edge of the wood though the ground was still rising. I left the last trees behind and ran on, my breath sobbing through my open mouth, my face a furnace the cool breeze couldn't quench. The track disappeared in grass and heather, the top of the rise was reached and twenty yards beyond I saw the sea, far below, stretched out like ink to a dim horizon. I slowed down, staggered to the edge and halted, gasping.

I was at the top of a great semi-circle of cliffs, descending like dark curtains to a cauldron in which the water surged untiringly, battering and sculpting the rock face hundreds of feet below. The shape of this gigantic basin brought the muted surge and deep crash of the waters to my ears as I stood there, sagging with exhaustion, my eyes drawn downwards. In the dim light from the few stars visible between the clouds, I decided vaguely that the pitch-black shadows hiding the cliffs indicated that the sea had deeply undercut the cliff-top. But it was only a fragmentary thought. More and more, a depressing numbness, a hopelessness of spirit was overwhelming me so that my weary brain was beginning to plead that it couldn't take any more, that it wanted rest, above all it desired oblivion.

The blin' shores o' Kilbrannan, in the mirky pit o' night—
Who said that . . .? What does it matter?

In a corner of my mind, something tiredly fought this mood, fought its insidious spread, its use of all the shocks I had been exposed to—the knowledge that I was hopelessly mentally disturbed, that I had killed Alison, the near certainty that Alan and his world were illusion half a year away from this winter's night, that Jane . . .

The edge was only a foot away: no one falling over could survive. It would be quick. One step, a short moment of relaxed falling through the rushing air and then oblivion. Take the step, the final decision and rest forever, all problems solved.

I took one last look at the sky. In a patch between black cloud-banks, high up, the northern cross of Cygnus glowed through slight haze with Altair's star trio also clear. I felt my head drawn downwards to the murmuring cauldron far beneath, perhaps I swayed forward, then the last remnant of rationality in me screamed in shocked realisation.

Cygnus. A summer constellation. Something blazed within me like a match struck in darkness. My head came up, my eyes staring. There it was. The cloud-bank to the left was beginning to hide one arm but everything else was visible. And the calendar on Ebor's desk said January 10th. It just was not possible to see Cygnus so high up in the sky in the depths of winter. I found I was thinking as Alan Ramsay now; the Peter Campbell *persona* still fought, displaying its memories like shopworn goods that have lost their charm, but it was not now coincident with consciousness. Then what the hell was wrong with me? My fingers touched the raised scab of the wound on the shaven part of my head. What tricks had been played on me? That reflection in the mirror? Where was I? Total bewilderment swept over me; a foot from my toes the grassy edge separated earth and space. I stepped back. I was Alan Ramsay. I saw the sun on the waters of the North Channel, Jane's profile, the wind stirring her hair, a sandstone cross, a harbour wall. Tears blinded me, scalding my eyes, sobs wrenched my chest as a turbulence of emotions swept over me—relief and joy, exultant, blazing, mingled with the beginnings of a confused rage and an implacable resolve to discover why I had been tormented and driven to the edge of sanity.

I turned away from the brink, shuddering at the narrow, fortuitous margin by which I had escaped destruction, still hearing as if in echo the insinuating persuasive promptings to jump. My rage took fire. I faced the outskirts of the wood and halted, a wave of shock freezing me.

A nearly-full moon, that up till now had been blotted out by cloud, slid from behind the bright-edged cloud-bank to reveal a dark, bulky figure standing between the nearest trees. I took several steps away from the edge, the rushing whispers of the waves receding, then stopped again as the figure loped forward, moonlight illuminating the white sweater and trousers. When he was ten feet from me, I recognised George, his teeth showing between his grinning lips.

He could be genuine, I thought confusedly, the cold sweat from my past mental conflict feeling chill on my trembling body; he could have been told I was a patient and now he means to take me back. But the fear he instilled in me must have alerted me at the last moment. Without breaking his stride as he ran towards me, he suddenly lashed out his right foot in a kick that would have doubled me up, totally incapacitated, in retching agony if it had connected. As it was, I was almost too late in jerking aside and his foot crashed into my left hip bone. If he had been wearing boots he might have crippled me; in fact his sandshoe left a burning bruised agony that aroused an outraged anger within me. He was frighteningly quick in his reactions. Before I could attempt flight, his hand grabbed my arm, tugged and his arms clamped themselves about me, imprisoning my own arms against my sides. He heaved me off the ground, turned and was shuffling towards the cliff edge with terrifying intent before I could react. In a frenzy of disbelieving fear, I wrapped my legs round his and he fell on top of me, my head out over the void, his body blackly outlined against the night sky. He raised himself, trying to disengage prior to pushing me over and I twisted my upper body aside, the crushed damp grass under my hair momentarily allaying the panic I'd felt when nothing supported my head. I got my right hand free and clutched the thick ribbed wool of his sweater, the hooked fingers of my left hand scrabbling at the roots of the tough grass. I poured all my strength into a push that shoved him to one side. The next moment we had scrambled to our feet to face each other, crouched, hands raised, conscious of the brink on one side of us and the grumbling, dashing sea far below in the darkness.

He jumped away from the edge then to put himself between me and safety. I glanced back. I was within five feet of the brink. When I flicked my gaze back to him I felt sick, my mouth metallic with fear. In his right hand he now held a knife, blade rising towards me.

Gradually he approached me while I took two wary steps forward, every nerve tingling, my heart thumping. His blade stabbed upwards towards my diaphragm. I jerked back, feeling the tug of the knife in my jacket, my hands whipped inwards, grabbing at his wrist and forearm and I threw myself backwards, landing on my seat. I doubled my knees to my chest then catapulted my feet up and out. They struck his falling body just below the waist, shot him over my head and I was turned over on my side, gasping, the smell of grass and damp earth and salt in my nostrils while a despairing yell died away in the blackness. Through my gasps, the distant surge was audible.

I sat up, pain flaming from my hip and listened. I couldn't believe yet he was gone. But the moonlight was sufficiently bright to let me see I had the cliff-top to myself. I sprawled, peering over the edge. Deep down in the great cauldron the moonlight whitened the seething turbulence, contrasting it with the black dinosaur teeth of rocks it boiled round. No one could have survived that fall. . . . *It was quick, a short step forward, and all problems solved . . . just let myself go.* With a shocked gasp I pushed myself back, crushing down the insidious suggestion.

I got up, groaning at the pain in my hip. A new pain gnawed at me and I explored my chest. Jacket and shirt had been slashed and a stickiness told me that the knife had sliced me shallowly. Since I did not seem to be bleeding much, I ignored it, trying to beat my brain into some sort of logical thinking. It was like trying to think with a dozen people yelling, cajoling, arguing in my ears.

How long would it be before someone else arrived? Had George been sent out to follow me, to make sure I threw myself over the edge? How in heaven's name could they know I'd take the path through the wood to the cliff-top when I jumped over the wall? Had I escaped before and come this way? I had no answer to these so I went on. Since I didn't commit suicide, George came forward to murder me. And then go back to Ebor? Patient cured, Doctor! My head began to throb. What would happen now? When George failed to return, would they send someone else, or would they wait until morning? I couldn't bank on that. I had to get away from here, wherever it was, and try to make sense of the whole devil's brew, try to distinguish illusion from reality. 'The world becomes a dream and the dream becomes a world'. Oh God, supposing this was still hallucination, the feverish nightmare of a sick mind; supposing I still lay in my hospital bed in troubled sleep and this sequence was a new construct, a device to discredit Ebor who only desired to heal me—if my mind could furnish a world in summer it could provide a constellation out of season; supposing I'd imagined George's murderous attempt and had in the real world attacked him—No! No! No! I clenched my fists.

This was reality—this had to be, the grass, the breeze, the cliff, the moon, the clouds, the wood, the pain, the blood. At least let me get away from here, let me put a few miles between this place and myself, let me find some hiding place in which to crouch and think.

I began moving away from the cliff edge, striking left as I faced the wood. Its outskirts did not quite reach the edge and I aimed for the gap. While the moon remained visible, I had little trouble in picking my way over the rough, grass-covered surface but occasionally a cloud hid it, deepening the darkness to such an extent that I had to step very warily and slowly for fear of falling into an unexpected cleft or wandering over the snaking cliff edge. The coastline and landscape were completely unknown to me and I doubt if I made much more than one mile per hour in the next three hours. I came to one small burn that tumbled down a rocky cleft; in daylight it would have taken a minute to cross. In the darkness, it took twenty minutes. I slithered carefully down one steep slope, clambered for some time along the shadowed rocks until I came to a narrow section where the water bubbled and chuckled unseen over a series of steps. With care I was able to feel my way across and struggle wetly up the opposite side.

After a period of time I estimated to be four hours, I was dead-beat. My left ankle ached, the pain in my side had lessened but the strain of making progress over an unknown landscape in darkness had exhausted me. In addition the clouds now blotted out the moon. I clambered over a dry-stane dyke, stumbled into a shallow hollow covered with heather and grass, and sank to my knees. Lying down I thought dazedly: if I'm right and it is summer, it must be about 2 a.m. and it'll be dawn in four or five hours' time at the most. If I'm wrong and it *is* winter and only about 10 p.m. now, it'll be a long, long night until dawn, ten or more hours away. But whichever it is, no one's going to find me here.

I closed my eyes and sought for sleep. It was not a deep or restful slumber I fell into. My brain was too active, too feverish. Fragments of memory and pseudomemory—how I wished I knew for certain which was which—furnished me with images, visual and aural and tactile, mixed up, garish, presented in no order. I refought George on the cliff top; again he fell over, his despairing scream echoing in my head; again I sprawled face down at the edge, trying to see the boiling ocean below but now to my horror his white hand came up and gripped mine, his face with staring eyes and fixed grin appeared above the edge and he began to drag me over into the abyss—I woke up screaming and half-sat up in the darkness, shuddering, feeling the rough heather under my hand and the cool night air on my streaming face. I lay back, trembling, my eyes turned to the Pole Star. I forced myself to relax, to identify the stars in the Plough, to separate the double star Mizar, then trace the rough W of Cassiopeia across the Pole from the Plough, until sleep came again, troubled, uneasy but unbroken now until my eyes opened to the morning light and the waving heather and grass stalks a few inches from my face.

11 Not any port in a storm

I lay still, changing the focus of my eyes from the stalks to the grassy rise beyond. Gingerly, I allowed my mind to awaken to activity, almost as if it were an engine with a faulty gear-box. Who am I? I am Peter Ca—No! Alan Ramsay. Unpleasant, hollow sensation and a spurt of jumbled memories as if a mill-lade had been opened momentarily in my brain. But my personality was more coherent now, surer of its identity as Alan Ramsay, better able to form an opinion as to the genuineness or counterfeit nature of a particular memory, more confident. I was far from being back to normal mentally; my mind was like a bicycle rider who, having had a dazing, damaging spill from his machine, had picked himself up, remounted his battered bike and was now weaving his way unsteadily along the road, on the verge of falling more than once but gradually regaining his strength, his skill and his confidence. And through all my mental activity now, a red thread of anger ran.

I turned over and sat up cautiously, my body stiff and sore, and examined my chest. There was a six-inch slit in the cloth of the grey jacket, not really noticeable, a tear in the shirt, which stuck in one place to the wound. It couldn't have been deep since there was very little dried blood on the shirt. But if that knife had slashed up one inch nearer—I wondered if Ebor had gone to the cauldron last night after George failed to return or if he had decided to leave it till daybreak. In the darkness he wouldn't have been able to see anything; remembering my view of the boiling chaos of water crashing over the wet jagged rocks, I didn't think there was much chance even in daylight of discovering anything. I thought it likely any body would have been swept away. And so Ebor would have the choice of thinking that both George and I had gone over—improbable, or that George alone had gone over and I was wandering about—even less likely, or—what? I hoped he was a worried man.

I raised myself to my knees and scanned the horizon. For a line of beaters hoping to flush you from cover? part of me scoffed. Another, more sober part of me replied: is it impossible? But there was no human being in sight. I rose to my feet.

The landscape, predominantly in shades of green, with dun patches, formed a shallow bowl with low hills on every side so that the sea was hidden. The ground was moorland, hill-sheep country and I got the impression that I was a good few hundred feet above sea-level, though this may have been due to the fact that the cauldron had seemed hundreds of feet deep and I didn't think I had gone all that distance downhill. Across to my right was the cleft dug out by the garbh allt or stream I had crossed. And beyond it was the wood—my God, only about two miles away. So much for my judgement of distance covered in darkness.

Ahead of me, across half a mile of rising moorland, with isolated patches of gorse and bracken, was a small cottage, white-walled, with a dark grey slate roof. A dry-stane dyke enclosed a garden area and a dirt road marched up the hill witb an extension of the dyke to cross the shoulder and disappear. I wondered if it met anything resembling a main road. As far as I could see, I had never been in this part of the world before.

I glanced towards the sun, well up in the sky from the horizon, then looked back at the area of crushed grass I had used as a bed. Remembering the direction in which I had seen the Pole Star, I reckoned the sun to be roughly north-east, an impossible direction if it had been winter and I was still in the Mull of Kintyre. I felt my lips tighten.

The time was probably past nine o'clock and I had slept until now because of mental and physical exhaustion and doubtless because the hollow in which I had lain had kept me in the shade until a few minutes ago.

The cottage seemed the most sensible goal so I began to walk stiffly towards it. If it was inhabited I could probably find out where I was, and the date. I stuck there: you don't usually knock at anyone's door and inquire what the date is. On my way across the moor, I tried to decide just what I should tell them. I had not really decided when I reached the dyke enclosing the garden.

Running a hand through my hair and straightening my jacket, which in fact fitted me quite well though I had no recollection of ever buying it, I knocked at the green-painted door. It was opened by a young woman wearing a long, old grey sweater, patched jeans and open-toed sandals, her fair hair swept back in a pony-tail held by an elastic band. She looked enquiringly at me.

'I seem to have lost my way. Can you tell me where I am?'

'You're near Glenehervie.'

The name meant nothing to me and my face must have shown this for she said: 'Where are you making for?'

A good question. I took a chance.

'Southend.'

'That's quite a distance. About six or seven miles.'

A feeling of relief swept over me.

'Which direction should I take?'

'The track behind the cottage will take you to the road. Turn left and . . .' She broke off, her eyes troubled. 'Are you hurt?'

I glanced down. Above the vee of my jacket the blood-stain was visible.

'I fell crossing the burn last night. A sharp rock.'

'You mean you've been out all night?' Her voice was startled, concerned.

'Well, yes.'

She frowned. 'You must come in. You'd better get that attended to.'

I protested but she insisted. The door opened immediately into a large, old-fashioned kitchen-cum-living-room, comfortably untidy. There was a fire in a black iron range, and a kettle steamed on the hob. The beamed ceiling was low. A massive oak dresser stood along the wall opposite the fireplace, a table and chairs occupied the centre of the room and under the window was a sink. There was a second door opposite the entrance. On a rug on the floor a plump baby newly at the crawling stage was zestfully bullying a patient black and white collie.

I was ushered into one of the two, worn armchairs on either side of the range while the girl went for a basin. I glanced round and noted a guitar on the dresser. Beside me on the stool was a stack of books. I smiled at the baby. It sat solemnly inspecting me, its thumb in its mouth, its other hand buried in the collie's fur. The collie lay, chin in paws, grateful for the respite.

The baby's mother poured water from the kettle into the red, plastic basin, went to the sink, added some cold water from the tap, then fetched a big square Huntley and Palmer's biscuit tin from the top drawer of the dresser.

'First aid box,' she said. She placed them on the table, having cleared a space by pushing aside dishes and, to my astonishment, a red woollen undergraduate gown.

'Glasgow?' I asked, pointing to it.

She looked at it and grinned before throwing it on to the sideboard.

'Yes. I'm getting more use out of it now down here. It comes in handy for wrapping the baby in, or myself last winter when I was up at night feeding him. Now, you'd better patch yourself up while I make some tea.'

I stood up and edged out of my jacket, musing at the trusting, motherly nature of the young woman. Getting out of my shirt was a tricky business. Finally I soaked the cloth she had provided with hot water and gradually eased the sodden shirt away from the wound. It burned dully and began to bleed a little. I washed it while the girl bustled about, pouring boiling water into a brown teapot, cutting rolls and buttering them, putting two eggs in a pan with some of the boiling water before placing it on the range.

'How is it?' she asked, darting a glance at me.

'Not bad. I'll put some of this Elastoplast on it.'

I did so and replaced my shirt and jacket. At her suggestion I sat down at the table and had breakfast. The eggs, the rolls, the tea made possibly the best meal I have ever tasted. I told her I was at Glasgow and we chatted about the University, various members of staff and some of the customs. She poured herself a cup of tea. Evidently she had taken an Arts degree; her husband had studied agriculture. They had decided to take on this place for a year or two until he had acquired practical knowledge of sheep and she tested her liking for the farming life. Then they would let her father, who I gathered was well-to-do, finance them in buying a farm. She was attractively natural and open about it all and I congratulated myself on my luck in wandering into her care. Her calm acceptance of me without asking awkward questions was likewise fortunate.

I was having a third cup when the outside door opened.

'Sheena? I was talking to two fellows looking for a patient...'

I swung round. Framed in the doorway was a tall, full-bearded young man in rough check shirt and corduroys tucked into knee-boots. His mouth closed and he came into the room, his eyes fixed on me. I rose to my feet.

'Sandy, this gentleman lost his way last night and spent the night in the open. This is my husband, Sandy McKillop. I'm sorry, I didn't get your name.'

'Alan Ramsay.' I could read his mind as if I were telepathic. He scanned the girl, the baby, the dog to see if they were unharmed. He had obviously been told to watch out for me and was considering his next move. I wondered if he'd been told I was dangerous.

'Oh yes.' He had a Glasgow accent. 'And how did you manage that?'

'I've never been to the Mull before and since I had a couple of days off I thought I'd wander about. I'm also keen on geology and I'm afraid it led me off the beaten track yesterday evening. And then I fell. I must have knocked myself out. When I recovered consciousness, it was dark.' It sounded the most appalling tissue of lies and his face showed it. To my dismay I found he was staring at a point just above my left ear. I hastened on.

'Your wife has been most helpful and I'm very grateful. She tells me I can get on to the Southend road at the end of the lane?'

He hesitated. 'Yes, that's right.'

I saw then that he wanted me out of the house, away from his wife. There would probably be an explosive row after I'd gone for it was obvious he was tensed up, ready to move if I ran amok or behaved in any way threatening. Of course, once I was on my way, he might well run for help. Which reminded me.

'By the way, I don't suppose you have a phone?'

'No.' I believed him; if he'd been lying his wife's face would have shown it. Afraid of being too abrupt, he added: 'No, we don't find any need of it.'

'Ah well, I'm not expected back anyway until tonight. I'll get on my way then. Thank you again, Mrs McKillop.' I turned towards her and halted. I was facing a large mirror fixed above a small bureau to the left of what I took to be the bedroom door. Looking out at me was Peter's face, above a grey dressing-gown with scarlet piping. The fabric of my mind, that I had so laboriously rebuilt, crashed in a flood of gnawing self-doubt and raw terror. I felt the blood leave my face, my stomach churn the food I'd consumed. I rubbed the sweat from my upper lip in one convulsive movement and stifled a sob as the reflection's grey-clad arm did likewise.

I mumbled: 'It's been good of you,' and walked stiffly out past the shepherd, my eyes unseeing. Somehow I got round the little cottage and on to the track. I began to climb the slight rise, my brain struggling to achieve calmness, to hammer down icy fears that the scene in the mirror was reality while all else, hills, cottage, the shepherd and his wife, were a chimera, a solipsistic creation. Solipsism. Logically unassailable, emotionally unsatisfactory. Who said that? Ah yes, dear old Ramon, goddam him. For he had to be in it too. And Dorothy West. But my carefully nursed flicker of anger, encouraged to protect me against the icy blast of terror, dwindled momentarily as I warned myself that the cry 'the whole world's against me' was itself symptomatic of mental instability.

I reached the top of the rise and looked back. No one had come out of the cottage. And there was no one else in sight. Ahead of me the track curved downhill to join a better road, single-tracked but surfaced. It wound its way in both directions between the hills. I began to walk as fast as I could. With no telephone in the shepherd's cottage I reckoned that it would take him half an hour or more to summon help. And in any case he might not be too keen to leave his wife alone in the cottage.

When I reached the surfaced road I turned left. The sun was so warm now that I took off my jacket and slung it over my left arm. I strode along, continually scanning the rolling fields and moors. I had gone perhaps half a mile when the distant sound of a car engine brought my head round. I badly needed a lift but I didn't want one from Ebor. On the left side of the road the grass verge fell away sharply. I climbed down so that I was concealed and looked back along the road to where it disappeared round the shoulder of a hill. The engine note grew louder and a van turned the corner. I hesitated, my mind dithering, then as it approached I saw it was a travelling shop. Scrambling into my jacket and buttoning it up to conceal the bloodstains, I jumped up on to the verge. My waving arms brought the cream-painted van to a halt feet from me. As I went forward to the offside of the van I found myself thinking of the terrified man who'd stopped me near Keprigan. The van driver leaned out.

'You want a lift?'

'Yes, please. Are you going into Southend?'

'Yes. Hop in.'

The accent proclaimed him Italian. I slid in to the front passenger's seat and looked through the gap in the partition behind us. The sight of stacked rows of breakfast cereals, detergents, groceries, vegetables and fruit was very reassuring.

He had a round, olive face, glossy hair and dark, good-humoured eyes. Over a faded pullover and trousers he wore a brown linen coat. Evidently he made this trip three times a week from his shop in Southend to all the outlying farms and cottages in the Mull of Kintyre south of the Campbeltown–Machrihanish line.

I asked him how long he'd been doing it.

'Eighteen years. I worked on a farm down here during the war. When I was sent back to Italy, conditions were bad and I found I kept thinking of the people here and so I came back.' He smiled happily, his eyes on the winding road ahead. 'I married a Southend girl and now I have three children. Two boys and a girl.'

By now I had deduced that I must be on the Learward road. In which case the Institute I had escaped from could not be the David Campbell Neurological Institute near Keprigan. I puzzled over that one even as I realised that the sea was now visible about a mile ahead and that we were descending towards Benton Polliwilline. Three miles out, I saw Sanda Island with Sheep Island a little nearer. And Macharioch Bay, with the stone cross on its headland and the beach where Jane and I had watched the sea birds, would be just over a mile away. A warm feeling flooded over me.

I wondered what Ebor was doing. I had to assume that he and his friends would keep searching for me once they learned from the shepherd that I was still alive. What would they think I would do? Try to contact Jane, Peter, the Outstation people, the police? I could phone any of them, or visit them. Ebor could, if he had sufficient men, picket these places (would Jane be at her house or at the Institute?—I couldn't tell since I didn't even know what day of the week it was), but he could do nothing about a phone call. It appeared that he had absolutely no scruples where human life was concerned but before he could do anything to prevent me hitting back, he had to find me.

While Toni attended to customers at a farm, I sat in the front seat and sweated it out. Quite suddenly I realised with a surge of relief that my brain was working more smoothly and efficiently than it had been since I recovered consciousness in that damned building, wherever it was. It was not now a case of: I had my brain washed last night and I can't do a thing with it. I reckoned it was now about half an hour since I had left the shepherd's cottage. I decided I could stick with Toni until he reached Southend.

He took the travelling shop this morning along the branch of the road to the north of the Corachan Burn as he did every other trip. Ultimately we crossed the Conieglen Water at the mill and reached the main Campbeltown–Southend road.

His shop lay at the Dunaverty end of the village. I thanked him, got out of the van and walked on a few yards until he had disappeared indoors. Very carefully I searched the road, the fronts of the houses for anything suspicious. As far as I could see, the few people about were either inhabitants or holidaymakers.

I now began to follow the road westwards towards the shore, feeling horribly exposed and vulnerable since there was absolutely no cover on the seaward side and only a rising slope on my right with the occasional building. I passed High Keil and the technical school ruins. At Keil Point, where the road turned inland round the hill, I climbed over the fence and took to the shore. Apart from cutting the distance by almost two miles, my route bypassed Jane's cottage at Carskiey and a possible Ebor picket. Trees and other obstacles prevented anyone at the cottage from seeing the coast.

I crossed the mouth of the Breackerie Water by the bridge, crossed the Strone Water where it enters the Breackerie and trudged along the coastal track in the direction of the cliffs. Four hundred feet above me and hidden from view, the hills brought the road to the Gap and the Kintyre lighthouse to within three hundred yards of the coast. A quarter of a mile further on, I reached the foot of the eastern cliff sheltering Port Mean.

It was not too difficult a climb to the top. Its almost sheer rampart was broken up into rough steps and stairs clothed with tufts of coarse vegetation affording handgrips. I carefully avoided looking down. When I scrambled up on to the top, I lay prone on the heather, gasping until I recovered. The bruise on my hip-bone was aching and the slash on my chest nipped. But my head was definitely clearer.

I stood up. Far below me the houses and harbour of Port Mean formed a toy seaport in a green bowl. I noted that the harbour basin was empty of fishing boats though a few holiday craft brought splashes of colour to the water. The narrow road curved down the far slope of the bowl, houses on either side at the foot, and ended at the square. I took a deep breath before moving on. A few yards beyond me was the ruin of a World War II lookout station, its grey, mouldering concrete unsightly and almost overgrown, twisted rusty metal bars sticking out of it. Further on, a narrow path through the ferns and bracken seemed to lead downwards towards the Port. I began to follow it down the inside of the bowl. Ten minutes later I was approaching the outlying cottages on the eastern side of the Port.

Two middle-aged women gossiping outside a house gave me the information I required. I was conscious of their laser-like gaze on my back as I went down the cobbled lane they had indicated. Their wildest speculations about my business would fall far short of reality. Fifty yards along the lane I came to my goal and rattled the black iron ram's-head knocker on the burnt sienna door. Thirty seconds later it opened and Korky looked up at me. His lined features relaxed in a smile.

'Well, well, if it isn't my nervous friend. Come in, come in.'

12 An end to it all

I sat in an armchair, my hands gripping the polished ends of the curved wooden arms, and took a deep breath.

'Would you answer me three questions, Korky?'

He sat opposite me, his stick resting close at hand.

'Only three?'

'Three to begin with.'

'Fire away.' Was it my imagination, or did he seem unnaturally watchful?

'Firstly, who do you think I am?'

He didn't say 'That's a damn fool question' or ask me if I didn't know my own name.

'As far as I know, you are Alan Ramsay.'

I felt my chest heave and the cut protested.

'What date is it?' According to the wag-at-the-wa' clock the time was twelve-fifteen.

'Friday, July 10th.' It had been the morning of Tuesday, July 7th, that I had called at the Institute. Tuesday, Wednesday and most of Thursday had been snatched out of my life. My brow wrinkled and the fingers of my left hand gingerly rubbed the rough scar in the clearing among my hair. I bared my teeth in a grimace.

'Have you a mirror?'

Without a word, he got up and limped out of the room while I sat there, cold fury surging within me. When he returned, he carried a round shaving mirror about the size of a side-plate.

'Best I can do.'

I took it and hesitated. Mirror, mirror, on the wall, can't you see my face at all? With a distinct effort I turned it and looked into it, cheek muscles rigid. The reflection swirled, melted, re-formed, was Peter's face one moment then my own the next, for all the world as if the mirror was one of those trick 3-D pictures where the image seen depends upon the angle of viewing. I screwed my eyes up then re-opened them. It was my reflection I saw then, complete to the slightly bent nose and the tiny scar bisecting the right eyebrow. Relief made me sag back. I handed the mirror to Korky with trembling fingers. He put it on the mantelpiece.

'Do you realise,' he said mildly, 'that half the Mull of Kintyre—including the police—have been looking for you for a week? And a certain young woman is more than slightly perturbed because you left no forwarding address?'

I felt my face flush.

'Jane?'

'Who else? Of course it may be the Mull is stiff with girls you know . . .' He broke off. 'Incidentally, when did you last eat?'

'About three hours ago.' I suddenly realised I was hungry.

'M'ph'm. I'll put the kettle on. I take it you mean to tell me what's been happening to you?' He got up and crossed to the sink under the window looking out on to the lane, filled a kettle and put it on to the electric cooker. For the first time I began to relax enough to take stock of my surroundings. It was a comfortable, neat little living-room, brightened by the profusion of potted, semi-tropical plants standing round the walls.

'I wish I could,' I said. 'Most of it is a blank and I'm not sure you'll believe what I do remember.'

'Try me.' He brought out saucepans and used a can-opener on tins of Campbell's soup and Ambrosia Rice. 'Not cordon bleu cooking, I admit, but then it's an easy recipe to follow and anyway at the moment the food is incidental.'

While he prepared the meal, I described the Tuesday

morning events, which now seemed so remote, then told him of my experiences since I regained consciousness on what I now knew had been Thursday evening about 10 p.m. By the time I'd finished, we had taken our places at the table, eaten the soup and rice and were drinking tea. He had listened attentively, interrupting twice only, to get me to enlarge on my mental state at one point and to try to locate more precisely the position of the shepherd's cottage. He didn't seem shocked, even when I described how I'd killed George.

'And that's it,' I concluded.

He ran a thin hand over his sparse, sandy hair.

'Well, it's quite a story. A bit improbable. No! Hear me out. You can produce no proof of your story. Even if you show me a cut on your chest and a bruise on your hip-bone, that cannot count as evidence. And, you see, I really know nothing about you other than what I learnt at the ceilidh or from Jane since or my impression this past hour. That's what's got to be faced.' I felt bitterly disappointed and absurdly indignant, even though I could not fault his logic. But he wasn't finished. 'Seriously, what do you think the police would make of a yarn like this? Eminent brain surgeon aided by distinguished foreign doctor and the housekeeper of the local lady of the manor, kidnap for no known reason a scientist from a tracking station, hold him prisoner while they brainwash him in an incredibly short space of time into believing he is someone else and drive him to the point of suicide.' He paused. 'And when he baulks, try to murder him.'

I felt depressed. To the outside observer, which would be the more credible; that my story was true, or that in some way I was suffering delayed after-effects of my accident?

'What's the official theory about my disappearance?'

Korky hesitated, then shrugged. 'According to Jane, you left the Institute having had your stitches out and just drove away. When you didn't arrive back at your Out-station after a reasonable time, they made inquiries and got worried. Everyone's been looking for you since then. Very popular fellow you are.'

'I see. What about my car?'

'Sunk without trace.'

I'll bet. My mood of depression deepened. Already it would be implicit in the authorities' composite mind that I had flipped my lid. So that if I went to them and told my story they'd make soothing noises and do nothing. And my own people? They'd advise an extended leave.

No, somehow I had to make sense of it all by myself. And to do that I needed more information, more help. At least my decision to make for Korky's place at Port Mean had been a sensible one. It provided a breathing space. For the first time I felt a degree of confidence begin to grow within me. The immediate problem was how to get in touch with Jane. I could hardly toddle up to Keprigan and knock on the door and ask 'Is Jane coming out to play?' That way I'd end up with one of Ebor's scalpels in me.

I looked at Korky.

'Have you a phone?'

He shook his head. 'I'm afraid not.'

The phone bell rang. From behind the almost closed door on my left. My head turned swiftly, my eyes stared incredulously at the pale cream door even as the muffled 'burr-burr' continued. For one long sickening moment I feared my mind was playing tricks on me again then I turned back to Korky and realised my mistake. He still sat facing me but now he held an automatic pistol pointing at my chest. On his face was a curious mixture of regret and determination.

'As if on cue,' he said ruefully. 'Just stay still, Alan. I can't miss at this range.'

I felt dazed, almost completely disorientated, my mind stumbling and starting in confused efforts to re-assess the situation. Korky got carefully to his feet, grimacing in pain, left hand on his stick, right hand holding the gun trained steadily on me. The 'burr-burr' tone formed an insistent background to my whirling thoughts. He backed to the door, opened it, reached out behind the wall and lifted the phone. He brought it to his ear and listened.

'Yes. He arrived an hour ago . . . Yes, I'll keep him here

till you arrive . . . No, he knows. . . . No. It's all right. He won't get away. . .'

He replaced the phone, pulled the door over and limped back to his chair. An incredible thought formed in my mind.

'You knew I was coming here!'

'Yes. Dr Ebor told me.'

'When?'

'Let me see.' He rubbed his chin with his free hand. 'It must have been about nine o'clock this morning. They've been phoning at intervals ever since to check.'

I closed my eyes, the now familiar feeling of despair squatting like an incubus on my shoulder. As far as I knew, my decision to make for Port Mean and Korky's cottage had been taken while I sat in Toni's travelling shop. And that must have been long after ten. I forced a deep breath into my chest. What was the use of fighting, I thought dully, if they knew what my brain would decide even before it told me. Last night George had known I would turn left into the wood and go towards the cliff-top. For a wild moment I thought of the possibility of a radioactive tracer being implanted in my body—my fingers went up to touch the scar—then I knew this was not feasible. Or a tiny radio beacon powered by a biologically energised battery . . . ? Oh, don't be ridiculous. It would have to operate backwards in time to enable Ebor to predict my twists and turns.

Considering the problem like this came to my aid. Every scientist must have more than his fair share of obstinacy, persistence, pig-headedness, thrawn-ness, call it what you will, the ability that makes him go on tackling a problem, week after week. I began to feel anger again, first step towards recovery.

'How long before they arrive?'

Korky shrugged. 'Fifteen minutes or so.'

'Do you realise they'll kill me?'

Was there a slight tightening of his face muscles?

'Dr Ebor said they would not harm you. They would take care of you.'

'They've already tried to push me over a cliff.'

'So you say, Alan.'

'But, Korky, what earthly reason would I have for lying?'

'Dr Ebor says you want to injure him.'

'For God's sake, Korky, make sense. I hadn't met Ebor until a week ago. At the ceilidh I told you where I work. Jane must have told you about me.'

The lines on his face deepened. I pressed on.

'Jane's been worried about me since I disappeared. You said so yourself. Where do you think I've been?'

'Wandering about, I suppose. Dr Ebor said they picked you up last night. You were delirious, raving about some fantastic experiments he was supposed to have performed on you and how you were going to get your revenge. He said you were violent and that you attacked one of his staff. He said you hoped to hide here. I'm sorry about the gun but I have to detain you until Dr Ebor arrives.'

'But this is a complete pack of lies.'

'I doubt if Dr Ebor would tell lies.'

I felt as if someone had replaced my blood with ice-water. I found it impossible to reconcile this Korky with the tolerant, amusing, intelligent Korky of the ceilidh. It was almost as if . . .

'Let me phone Jane, Korky. Before they arrive.'

'I don't want Jane hurt, Alan. You might say things that would distress her.'

I took a tight grip of myself, forcing down the desire to yell at him. I glanced at the clock, feeling my forehead wet.

Korky was still watching me. I had to be missing something. There had to be some reason why I had been considered a suitable case for treatment. I tried to re-run my visit to the Institute to get the stitches out. My accident memories had returned because I saw the photograph. That technician was the one who stopped my car on the Keprigan road. It had to be something to do with that. He had been terrified. And there had been a second man. And I had actually been out of the car, standing beside it when —well, when everything went black.

What was the technician's name? The sister had told

me. Kerr, no Carr. Innes Carr. That was it. I was sure I had never met him before the encounter on the Keprigan road. But the name produced a sort of echo. I repeated it, several times. And then I got it. As I sat there, leaning slightly forward in my effort to make sense of it all, bits and pieces from the past eight days began to come together, as if they had a life of their own, as if unseen lines of force connected them, manipulating them into their correct positions in my mind, like the orderly, mysterious, meaningful movement of chromosomes in a fertilised cell; something Peter had said, something Korky himself had mentioned only a moment ago, a statement by Ramon himself. And so on. There were bits missing, matters I had to guess about; other questions still went unanswered but I had a nebulous theory now and like all theories it predicted certain things. And some of these things could be checked.

I looked at the clock again. One-thirty.

'Listen, Korky, I know you have no grounds for believing me but I think I've just got a glimpse of the truth. My theory may be pure fantasy—in one sense I hope it is because it has very unpleasant possibilities; in another sense I hope not because I have no other explanation to offer. But I need more facts. In particular I must see Jane.'

'Do I get to know what your theory is?'

'Yes.' I hesitated. 'Yes, I'll tell you.' I wondered uneasily if he would dismiss it as the incomprehensible produce of a disordered mind. He sensed my reluctance.

'Try it on the dog,' he grinned. For a moment he was the Korky of the ceilidh again. 'I used to have a Colonel who read every order he made to a particular major. "If Morrison understands it, anyone can," he'd say.'

'All right.' As I talked, the explanation lost some of its skeleton outline, became more substantial. Other events from the past week became incorporated with it. Korky's face reflected his close attention; soon other emotions were involved, astonishment, anger and, somewhat to my surprise, fear bordering on terror. Once or twice he wiped his face with a handkerchief.

When I had finished, he sat silent for a space of at least

half a minute while a titanic struggle went on within him, a struggle visible in his tortured eyes and glistening forehead.

'Korky,' I whispered. 'Think of Jane. What earthly reason is there for keeping her in the dark when she's got to know sooner or later? Let me phone her now.'

Above all else, I thought, I had to make her understand or at least warn her.

'Donald Mackay,' Korky said surprisingly. 'Donald Mackay.'

He sighed and lowered the pistol and my heart leapt.

'I'm not up to a lot of the things you've told me,' he said, 'but I think you may well be right. You could be wrong in a number of details but in outline I am afraid you're right. And if so . . .'

'And if so, there's been one murder already, if not two and there could be others.'

'M'ph'm. Not only of the body but of the mind.' A kind of shudder passed through his frail body. 'The mind itself. Alan . . .'

'Yes?'

'You say we need more facts?'

'Yes.'

'Well, we can get those. But you also say you must see Jane.'

'Yes.'

'You are sure she is not involved with them?' His face was troubled, drawn, but it was the old Korky now. He had won his battle, at least for the moment.

My first reaction was an angry denial. Indeed my mouth was open before I halted, caught up in a mixture of emotions and thoughts. It was partly self-doubt, engendered perhaps by the way my mind had been tampered with, a distrust of my own brain-processes that I feared would recur for some time yet. And then I remembered her face and the sunshine and the things we had talked about and I was completely if irrationally certain.

'No,' I said. 'She is not in with them.' I hesitated, then added: 'At the same time I should tell you my opinion isn't worth very much for I'm afraid I'm in love with her.'

His face relaxed; a warm spark entered his eyes.

'My own opinion tallies with yours, though I'm not sure it's worth much more for'—he shrugged ruefully—'I'm quite fond of her myself. But anyway, let's stick to that opinion. The question is, what do we do next?'

'We,' he had said. I drew a deep breath. I was no longer alone.

'We've got to contact Jane and meet her somewhere. Apart from the information and help she can give us, I don't like the idea of her being in that damn Institute with Ebor and Ramon, now that they know I'm still alive.' I remembered the fake report on Peter Campbell and felt my scalp tighten. 'And that I love her. They might try to use her as a lever.'

Two car doors slammed up the lane. I jumped up. Korky got to his feet.

'Lay the table over on its side. Quickly! And the two chairs.' And before I could stop him, he had raised the gun and clubbed himself on the jaw. The thud alone told me how painful it must have been. I lowered the table to the floor, followed it with the chairs. Korky passed me the gun then lay down on the floor as if unconscious.

'Go on. Out the back. Find a hiding place. I'll tell them you got away a minute after they phoned. And had previously said before I produced a gun that you intended to make for the Outstation. I'll call you in when they go.'

'We could take them with this?' I lifted the gun.

'And what then? March them to the police? We're not ready for that. We need time. Now go, for God's sake!'

It made sense and I rushed through the doorway he had indicated. There was a tiny garden neatly planted with banks of saffron marigolds, white roses on a pergola and wine-red dahlias. High brick walls separated the garden from its neighbours. Fortunately the door in the opposite wall was unlocked. When I opened it I found myself in a dirt lane, completely overgrown by a matted tangle of shrubs, trees and brambles, rising at the other side of the lane ever more steeply to form the eastern bastion of the Port.

I ran along the lane past three gardens before diving deep

into the concealing undergrowth. Sitting down I listened to my pounding heart, the dank earthy smells filling my nostrils. After a minute I put the pistol in my trouser pocket and wiped the sleeve of my jacket across my forehead.

Time passed. I wondered how Korky was managing. With the blow he'd given himself there would be a nasty contusion, quite conspicuous. He had shown remarkable presence of mind. Of course we needed more evidence and therefore more time. At present we really had nothing but suspicions and my completely unsubstantiated statement. But given time and a bit of luck we could present something that might make the authorities take action. Two feet in front of my nose I watched a fly struggling exhaustedly in a web spun among some bramble twigs. The spider came out from behind a leaf and tightroped towards its victim. I wondered what feelings, if any, a fly had in such circumstances and impulsively I brushed everything to the ground and stamped it into the earth.

Half an hour must have passed by now. I began to worry. Surely they'd've gone by now? And yet Korky hadn't come out. Could he have been swayed back to their side? No, absurd; if so he would have told them where to find me. Perhaps the tension and excitement—and the blow he'd given himself—had really caused him to pass out. I decided I'd have to go in and see.

I slithered down on to the path. There was no one in sight. I walked along the track to the garden door and pushed it open slowly, my other hand holding the pistol. The garden was empty. There was no one visible at the bedroom window beside the back door. I walked up the path, my stomach tight, the gun now raised before me and listened at the back door. Silence. I licked my lips and turned the knob. Having opened the door an inch, I listened again. There was no sound whatsoever. I pushed the door back, tiptoed along the short corridor to the living-room and halted.

Not only had table and chairs been set up again but the crockery had been picked up and, I saw wonderingly, been washed and replaced on the shelves above the dresser. Something made me turn and stare at the bedroom door.

It was half open. It had been closed when I left. I went to it and entered. Around the walls was more evidence of Korky's interest in semi-tropical plants. On the tops of a dressing-table and two small tables, rows of pots held delicate ferns, begonias, what I thought might be Japanese honeysuckle, and miniature cacti. But I ignored them.

On the bedcover lay Korky, his eyes closed, arms by his sides, his shoes by the end of the bed. There was a white envelope beside his left hand. I took two quick steps forward and felt for a heartbeat. There was none. When I pulled up an eyelid, the dilated pupil made no response to light. I rushed back to the living-room and fetched the shaving mirror. I held it close to his nose but there wasn't the slightest misting on it. He was dead.

With frozen, fumbling fingers I extracted a single sheet of paper from the unsealed envelope, addressed simply *To the investigating officer.*

Dear sir,

Having been in increasingly bad health for some years, I have decided to put an end to my life. The poison I am using is quick and painless. I got it some years back when I was out East. My possessions may be disposed of in any way seen fit.

I believe myself to be of sound mind in making this decision.

Yours sincerely,
Dugald I. McCorkindale

13 Dead man's clue

Stupid with shock, I found myself wondering what the 'I' had stood for. Then a sense of loss and guilt flooded over me. I had liked Korky: he had been a genuine person and now, by running out on him, letting him stay to face Ebor's men, I had as good as killed him. If I had stayed he probably would be alive at this moment. A small part of me protested that it had been the logical course of action to leave the cottage; a primitive, raw part of me dismissed the reason with bitter, flaying contempt.

I looked again at the note in my hand. I had no doubt that the handwriting was Korky's. In some way they had got him to write this letter—did he actually dutifully swallow the poison himself?—I felt sick at the thought—or did they force him to take the poison? In either event I knew Korky had not committed suicide. This was murder. My face twisted as I tried to understand. Even if they felt he had failed them by allowing me to escape, it was wasteful—to be cold-bloodedly pragmatic about the matter—to kill him. By doing so they lost a man; it didn't teach anyone a lesson. But what it did show me, if I had required the demonstration, was how little any human being meant to them.

My eyes went back to Korky's still face. In death the lines seemed shallower; already he was brother to the waxen figures I'd seen in the library side-room of Borgadel House. With an effort I overcame my paralysis. Using the top of the bedcover I rubbed those parts of the envelope and note I had held, inserted the note in the envelope and laid it down. I turned and saw the telephone on a small table. On a shelf under the tabletop were two directories, one for Glasgow, the other for the Mull of Kintyre. I riffled through the latter until I came to Jane's Carskiey number. I picked up the phone and dialled. While the distant 'burr-burr' note sounded I stood looking at the masses of flowering plants, now possessing a funereal role enhanced by the way they surrounded the bed and its occupant.

A minute passed. I replaced the phone. It had been a faint chance at best. I searched the directory for the David Campbell Neurological Institute. When I found it I picked up the phone again, hesitated, then dialled.

'David Campbell Institute.' The woman's voice was calm and pleasant.

'Is it possible for me to speak to Dr Selkirk?'

'Who is calling?'

'Her brother.'

'Just hold on please and I'll call her.'

I wondered if like many hospitals nowadays the staff carried their own tiny receivers in their coat pockets so that they could be asked to go to the nearest phone. I felt my scalp crawl when the thought hit me that the nearest phone could well be in Ebor's office.

The alive hiss seemed to last an eternity before I heard the switchboard operator's voice again.

'You're through now.'

'Hullo?'

'Hullo, this is Jane. Is that you, Martin?' Her voice sounded as if she had been hurrying.

Could anyone listen in on an extension? In some internal telephone systems this was possible though not in others. I had to take the chance that Korky had persuaded Ebor's men that I was now making for Low Glenadale and that they had reported this. I licked my lips.

'Jane, listen to me. Are you alone?'

'Y-yes. But . . .?'

'Please listen. Do not speak. This is Alan. Don't speak. Listen!'

There was a gasp from the other end. I hurried on.

'Jane, I am all right for the moment. I am at Korky's place in Port Mean. Do you know it?'

'Yes.'

'Are you on duty?'

'Yes.'

'When can you get off?'

'At five-thirty. But . . .'

'Can you meet me here?'

'Yes.'

'Jane, I am in serious trouble and you are the only one who can help me. I am asking you to trust me. Even although I can tell you nothing at the moment. When I see you I will explain. Will you come? Just say "yes" or "no".'

'Yes.' My throat burned, a warm tightness invaded my chest at the unhesitating way she had replied. And then fear gripped me.

'On no account must you tell anyone that I have spoken to you. Above all, do not tell Ebor or Ramon or Peter. Do you understand?'

'All right.' More slowly this time and uncertainly, the note of bewilderment apparent. Oh God, I thought, I must sound as if I'm completely out of my mind. I gripped the phone as if I would crush it.

'I know it sounds crazy, Jane, but I'll explain when you get to Korky's cottage. Don't tell anyone. If anyone questions you about this phone call you must say it was from your brother, that he is arriving unexpectedly in Glasgow tomorrow on business and he wondered if you could have dinner with him. Something like that. Will you do that, please?'

'Yes . . .'

'Thank you.' My voice shook. 'I'd better ring off now. Remember, Jane, if you have any regard for me, come alone and don't tell anyone. Goodbye.'

'Goodbye.'

I replaced the receiver quickly before she could add anything. I found I was trembling in reaction to the effort I had put into convincing her. Going through to the living-room, I sat down in the old chair to the left of the fireplace and sank back, arms outstretched. A storm of speculations tormented me.

Even if Jane meant to come, the phone call may have been overheard. I could very well have endangered her by phoning. Or she could, believing I was suffering some kind of brainstorm, tell Ebor in all good faith in spite of my entreaties not to. It would, I knew, be the sensible, medical thing to do, certainly not to rush alone to meet someone who for all she knew could be violent. But I could only hope that I was not entirely mistaken in believing she was fond of me and so would, against all rational thought, be swayed by her feelings to carry out my instructions. I wondered how she would get through the rest of the afternoon. Two-thirty-five. Probably three and a half hours to go unless she managed to get away a little early. And then my stomach contracted and I gripped the hard unyielding wooden arms.

If they had known last night I would turn left towards the cliff and that I'd make for Korky's place this morning, having escaped the cauldron, was it not possible they would know I'd decide to phone Jane, and that I would not try to get to the Outstation? Had I been programmed like a computer, a string of logical instructions having been fed into my brain: IF X THEN GOTO Y, ELSE Z. I couldn't be sure.

All I could do was to sweat it out. Jumping up, I began to search the cottage for anything of use. As I searched, with the ever-present knowledge nagging at me of what lay on the bed, my resolve hardened, tempered by the icy rage I now experienced.

In a tool-box under the sink, I found wire-cutters, a large hammer, a chisel and a screw-driver, all of which I laid on the table. Hanging from a nail at the side of the mantelpiece was a scuffed binocular case. I lifted it down. Inside was a pair of standard 7 x 50 Barr and Stroud naval binoculars. I fastened the case and put it beside the tools on the table. I took out the pistol and examined it.

With a shock I found it to be empty. I had to search several drawers before I found a full clip for it. Slamming home the clip in the butt, I halted, a splash of colour in the open drawer catching my eye. I pulled the drawer further open and felt my face harden. Among a clutter of other things I saw three medals, the Military Cross with its purple and white ribbon, the United Nations service medal, its blue and white striped ribbon clashing with the colours of a third decoration I didn't recognise. I glanced at the bed, my rage feeding energy into my limbs and I left the room.

On the back of the front door leading into the cobbled lane I saw a khaki canvas satchel. I put the tools and the binoculars into it, considered the pistol then stuck it in my trousers pocket. I was ready to go. Just about to open the door, I halted, frozen, when the knocker rattled. I tiptoed back into the bedroom and closed the door a moment before someone stuck his head round the outside door and called 'Are you in, Korky?' I glanced sideways at the quiet figure on the bed and thought, no, never again.

A second voice said: 'Maybe in the garden.'

'Aye, maybe. I'll just see.'

I heard him cross the living-room and open the back door.

'No, he isn't here.'

'We'll maybe find him at the harbour.'

The outside door thudded shut.

I waited for a minute before re-entering the living-room. The time was now five minutes to three. The lane was clear. I slipped out, closed the door and walked briskly up the lane, the canvas webbing of the satchel slung over one shoulder, the bag bumping my side. It hurt the large bruise so I switched it across.

Knowing the route this time I was able to reach the outskirts of Port Mean inside two minutes and began climbing up the steep dirt path towards the ruined World War II lookout post. Two hundred and fifty feet up, the track came to a little plateau, a temporary breathing-space among the ever-present brambles and tumbled grey rock slabs. I was high enough now. Selecting a convenient block of stone, with a larger one behind it to act as a back to my stone chair, I sat down. In front of me, the untidy, thorny bramble bushes gave me shelter from below.

Looking across the green and dun bowl to the far side,

I was in an excellent position to monitor everything coming down the narrow road curling over the eastern hill-slope, as well as any person approaching Port Mean across the rim by foot. All I had to do now was wait.

I judged it to be three o'clock.

Using the screw-driver, I scratched a white line on a grey horizontal slab in the sun's direction, then another intersecting it at an angle of forty-five degrees further north. When the sun lay in that direction it would be near enough six o'clock. One hundred and one things a Boy Scout can do, I thought mirthlessly. I chucked the screw-driver into the canvas bag and brought out the binoculars, focusing them on the distant road before placing them ready to hand.

During the long hot wait that followed, I re-ran several times my tentative theory, testing it as best I could for inconsistencies. I became more than ever convinced that I was right. There was very little traffic into or out of the Port to interrupt my train of thought, a few private cars, a lorry or two, only five people, obviously holidaymakers.

The sun's direction—the dazzling orb was just clear of the rise to my left—was not far from the second scratch when a splash of light caused me to jerk forward, swinging the binoculars to my eyes. This time it was Jane's pale blue Hillman Imp, now over the rim and descending the hill at rather too rapid a pace. At that range, with the glasses' magnification, I was able to see that the person driving was alone, though it was impossible to recognise her.

I sat still for a minute until the car disappeared behind the Port houses furthest up the hill. No other car came over the crest. Sliding the binoculars into their case and picking up the satchel, I began scrambling down the track, every ten seconds or so checking the road. I hadn't too much time but I knew the narrow, twisting Port Mean streets would slow any car to a crawl.

When I reached the corner of the lane I peered round it. For a moment I thought I was too late to intercept the driver of the Imp but seconds later Jane hurried round the corner. I let her get to Korky's door before I stepped round into view.

She wore a blue blouse and skirt, her head bare. When I appeared, she swung round, recognised me and her mouth opened. A look of questioning concern appeared, her right hand came forward and she sped towards me.

Jane, I thought, you idiot, you wonderful trusting idiot! I took her hand and found to my astonishment that it trembled. There was no one else about. I opened the door and drew her inside. Her expression was one of bewilderment now. We stood looking at each other for one long moment then somehow she was in my arms, I was holding her body pressed to mine, her hands clung to my back, we were kissing, small, quick, almost impatient kisses, my mouth moving over hers, my voice telling her what she meant to me, hearing her responses, assurances, murmured endearments. In wonder I saw tears glistening in her eyes, in joy I knew she did care.

At length she drew back, her hands on my upper arms, her eyes searching my face. I released her.

'You didn't tell anyone,' I stated, rather than asked.

'No one.' She looked around. 'Where's Korky?'

'Sit down, Jane. Let me explain first of all.'

She took the seat Korky had occupied. I began to tell her everything. It took some time. As I spoke her features expressed a bemused incredulity that found utterance when I related how Korky had produced a gun.

'Korky! Oh no! It's just not possible, Alan.'

Her face possessed a fierceness, exhibited a sense of outrage that confirmed my opinion of the man whose body lay next door. I continued, shrinking inwardly from the approaching moment when I had to tell her he was dead. When I did so she got up, her face drained of expression, and went into the bedroom. I followed her. Almost perceptibly, her training took over as she examined the body. At last she turned towards me, her face frozen and bleak, and we went back into the living-room. She sat down again, this time at the table, her slim forearms resting on it.

'I feel stunned,' she said. 'I believe you, Alan. It's like some frightful nightmare but it's real. It even makes sense.'

'Does it?' I thought of my own private nightmares of the past twenty-four hours. 'What happened to me, Jane?'

'Ramon must have put lysergic acid diethylamine in the drink he gave you. L.S.D. It need only have been a tiny dose. The hallucinations you described all point to this, the crossing of the sensory inputs—seeing lights when you're really hearing sounds, the inordinate attention to detail, the zoom lens effect, the primitive raw colours, the fragmentary break-up of a scene, and then the after effects, the misplaced emotions, paranoic suspicions. And possibly some other drug to knock you out.'

'And then?'

'They tried to convince you you were really Peter, mentally disturbed.'

'They damn near succeeded.' I shuddered.

'They must have gone to the most elaborate lengths.' She frowned. 'Even to preparing a false summary report you were "accidentally" allowed to read. And changing clock and calendar to set the stage to winter. And letting you see Dorothy West.'

'The false memories? How could they be planted on me?'

'Not too difficult. As far as possible they built on real memories—your crash, your knowledge of Peter's history, etcetera. Remember, they had full access to all your memories—they may well have used something like sodium pentathol on you. And they almost certainly induced a state of hypnosis by the electrode induction method and kept you in it while they inserted the false memories by suggestion probably repeated over and over again, hour after hour, in much the same way the advocates of learn-while-you-sleep methods do it—a tape-recorder and earphones.'

'But I saw that crash, I saw Alison catapulted through the windscreen.'

'I know. But you were under L.S.D.; it seems to facilitate the ability of the brain mechanisms responsible for the correlation of scenes, sounds, tastes, etcetera to memorise sense data coming via one channel, say the ear, in other modes, say as visual images. Haven't you ever in normal life remembered something and been quite unable to say whether you read it somewhere or were told it?'

'And Peter's image, in the mirror?'

'Post-hypnotic suggestion. They probably took you a number of times in those three days to that study and associated Peter's image with the mirror in the toilet. The trigger would be any large mirror. It'll wear off.'

'It has, effectively.' I watched her face. 'I suppose they also implanted the suggestions to escape, to go to the cliff, to jump, to make for here if I still existed.'

'Yes.' Distress touched her face. 'And they probably suppressed your true personality by some form of punishment, possibly by electric shock.' She frowned. 'That attendant. Describe him again.'

I did so as best I could.'

'That could have been Gonzales,' she said slowly. Her face cleared. 'Why, of course. You were taken to Kerran Lodge, Ramon's place. It's beyond Glenehervie. When he came here it was on the market and he bought it and installed two or three of his Armillans as servants. But why do all this to you, Alan?'

'Because I saw something I shouldn't. I saw the technician Innes Carr fleeing from them on the Keprigan road. In a last effort to escape he tried to stop me and get a lift. But one of them came up behind me and knocked me out. And probably Ebor or Ramon, knowing that concussion often destroys the memories of events just prior to an accident, took the chance that I'd forget the incident. If I did, it would be preferable to avoid causing an investigation into my death or disappearance. But since I did recover these memories, Ramon decided I'd better die.' Rage shook me like a dog shaking a rat. 'And I suspect that the elaborate way in which I was treated this past week was simply because I could be used as a guinea pig to test their brainwashing techniques before I was disposed of. I also suspect,' I added quietly, 'that I wasn't the first one.'

She glanced sharply at me.

'Yes, the technician.' I felt myself frowning. 'Do you remember the seance, Jane?'

'Yes.'

'Do you remember we taped it?'

'Yes.'

'Someone wiped that tape. They didn't want something that happened at that seance to be on record. I think that Dorothy West was the one who did it. And I think Ramon was really shaken by that seance.' I looked at her. 'Can you recall the words Alison called out when she went under?'

Jane's face tightened.

'Something about . . . "the world being shattered, water being cold".' She paused. 'Oh yes. "I'm drowning. Help me." And: "I'm in a car." No, that's not quite right.' The tip of her tongue appeared momentarily, moving between lips parted in concentration. 'No, it was: "car. I am in his car." Suddenly her eyes opened wide. ' "Carr. I am Innes Carr." '

I sighed.

'Yes. I think that's it, Jane. I think Alison, who is almost certainly psychic, somehow got that information. There's another bit to it, remember. She also said: "They're poisoning their minds. Stop them".'

'And you think Carr was destroyed by them?'

'I think it is highly probable he is dead and that only by the merest chance did I avoid following in his footsteps.' I wondered just what was the explanation behind Alison's bizarre experience. I could recall a score of similar events in the history of psychical research. Jane interrupted my train of thought:

'But if you're right, Alison could be in danger if they thought she would take part in other seances.'

'Yes. I wonder if it is significant that in the attempt on my mind they said Alison was dead.' I looked at the clock. 7.10 p.m. 'Carr was killed because he stumbled on to something that had been going on for almost a year. He was an electronics man, wasn't he?'

'Why yes. He was the best we had. But how did you know?'

'It had to be that.' I rose to my feet and slung the canvas bag over my shoulder. 'Let's go now, Jane. I think I can show you why Carr died, and Korky, and why Ebor and the others must be stopped.'

She got up and followed me into the lane, still bright with the evening's sunshine.

14 Programme for a captive audience

In the Hillman Imp she turned to me.

'Where are we going?'

'Borgadel House.'

The car engine fired and the vehicle bumped slowly over the cobbles. Jane concentrated on manœuvring the Imp round the narrow, twisting streets that had been laid down long before Mr Ford had dreamed up his first Model T. I sat nursing the tool bag, my eyes scanning for anything suspicious. I had to be right, I thought, the answer had to be found up there.

Coming over the crest out of the bowl, I saw the road junction ahead. A car was travelling eastwards but had obviously no interest in us. Jane swung the Imp sharp left; two hundred yards on, the wide open lodge gates of the house appeared. On my instructions, Jane passed the white board with its curt *Private grounds. No Trespassers* notice then turned the car off the gravel on to the grass, finally squeezing it into a deep tunnel of dark green rhododendron bushes so that it was completely invisible from the drive. We got out and checked that it was concealed and that there were no tell-tale earth scars on the turf.

The tools clinked in their bag so I wrapped it round them and held it in my left hand, feeling their hard tubular shapes through the rough canvas.

'It's not the house we're after, Jane, so let's go this way.'

I struck off through the undergrowth, Jane behind me. The bushes and trees, while providing good cover, were not too close together to impede progress and the ground underfoot was inches deep in the fallen, decayed twigs and leaves of past seasons. Probably less than ten minutes passed before I neared my goal. I slowed down as I came to the edge of the cover and saw the small stuccoed windowless building ahead with its tall trellis mast.

'There it is.'

Jane came to my side and looked out between two shrubs.

'But that's the TV repeater station for Port Mean.'

'Yes.'

It stood in a little clearing, completely hidden from Borgadel House except for the mast soaring above the pines and firs. I went up to the battleship-grey door. As I expected, it was locked. In addition, a padlock through a stout hasp provided even greater security.

I put down the canvas bag, opened it and went to work. By exerting maximum strength I managed to withdraw the screws from the plate holding the hasp. That took a good ten minutes. I now turned my attention to the lock. I hammered the chisel into the jamb at various points near the lock and levered. The wood splintered, raw wounds opening in it but the door still held. I felt sweat trickling down my face and glanced at Jane. Her face was white and tense.

Picking up the canvas bag, I emptied the tools out of it then folded it into a pad, tying it by its webbing over the door handle. I picked up the four-pound hammer, motioned Jane back and brought it up horizontally to the level of the handle. Gripping it two-fisted, I swung it back slowly, twisting my body as if it was a spring, then drove the hammer round with every erg of energy I possessed, aiming the massive head for the pad. The crash was muffled, the door juddered open, its lock shattered, the part in the jamb completely torn away.

For at least a minute we stood there, alert and waiting but the noise must have gone unheard. In our nervous state it had probably sounded much louder than it really was. I laid the hammer against the stuccoed wall. Among the trees the evening light was weak now and did little to illuminate the interior of the windowless structure. But it wasn't totally dark inside. A bluish, flickering light came from one corner of the room.

I felt round the edge of the doorway for the light switch. When the harsh glare of artificial light from neon tubes came on fully after the usual on-off hesitation, we entered the tiny room and I pushed the door to. We looked about us.

There should have been very little equipment present since ostensibly the repeater station merely consisted of a large aerial to accept the TV signals and a booster to strengthen the signal before it went into the coaxial cable piping it down the hill to the Port Mean houses. Certainly for that task there was no need to have what we saw.

On a bronze-tinted Handi-angle frame stood a cine-projector. There was a motionless loop of film in it. On another section of the frame was a television set, at right angles to the cine-projector. On its screen, the current episode of *Crossroads* was being acted out mutely. Both the TV set and the projector, via an angled semi-transparent mirror, were the targets of a television camera, also locked in the frame. It fed its output into a box I took to be the booster. A line carried the sound signal from TV monitor to camera. There were one or two other boxes of electronic tricks in the circuit. I supposed there had to be a filter in the main channel from the aerial set in parallel with the bypass circuit to block out the channel transmitting *Crossroads*. But in principle it was just what I had expected, ingenious yet simple, crude but effective. In any case, I thought, it's only a lash-up, a prototype. The refined one will come later, in another place.

'Who is supposed to look after this if anything goes wrong?' I asked.

'The Institute. Since it was provided by old Mrs Campbell and since the Institute has its own staff of electronics people here on the spot, it was thought best that we service it.' She frowned. 'Alan, that film loop . . .'

'Yes, that film loop. Do you remember some years ago some bright lads dreamed up what came to be called subliminal advertising?'

I saw by Jane's face that she did remember. I went on.

'It caused quite a stir at the time. Every twenty frames of a cinema film, you put in one exhorting the audience to drink Blogg's beer, or eat Crunchie-Crisps, or whatever you wanted to push. The cinema screen proclaimed the message once per second for a fraction of a second only, too short a time for it to be seen by any audience member consciously. But it was still a long enough time for the signal strength to be above minimum threshold and so it registered in the subconscious. The results of the experiments were a bit inconclusive but everyone knew that if the method could be improved, it was dynamite, not only where advertising was concerned but also where the freedom of the individual was at stake.'

'Yes.' She was still adjusting to it. 'Your critical faculties were bypassed.'

' ". . . and wicked dreams abuse the curtain'd sleep".'

She glanced sharply at me.

'And Ebor's been experimenting with this?'

'Yes. He and Ramon. Aided and abetted by Dorothy. She probably switched the film-strips regularly for them. The inhabitants of Port Mean have been the guinea pigs. Those with television and a preference for STV have been the subjects; those without TV or a preference for the other channels were the controls.' I grimaced. 'You know the expression "the suspension of disbelief". Where above all do most people apply it but in watching TV? The ordinary man's critical faculties are deliberately suppressed when he switches on.'

'The rumours?'

'Yes. No one found the rumour-monger for he was here.' I pointed to the cine-projector. 'God knows how much misery and mutual suspicion have been loaded on to the villagers by that. It caused at least one suicide, maybe more. And, of course, the acid test.'

She frowned.

'Donald Mackay, town wastrel and drunkard. No one with a good word to say for him. Yet he is elected with an overwhelming majority as county councillor. I wonder how many nights before the election the subliminal message "Vote for Donald; he's the best man for the job" was flashed on the TV screens in Port Mean. Unseen, of course. But there, hour after hour, night after night. Judging by their results, they've come a long way. I wonder if they've incorporated with their captions all those potent, meaningful psychedelic patterns discovered in the past few years.'

Anger flared within me as I pictured them standing above the little seaport, noting and assessing the bewildered inhabitants' behaviour, like vicious boys who have stirred up an ant's nest and entertain themselves watching the tiny creatures scurrying about trying to reduce the resultant disorder. This was the deadliest evil, the complete disregard of human beings' agony, the evil that had stained the twentieth century with obscenities such as the Final Solution.

'And Korky?' Jane's eyes held pain.

'I think Korky was their observer. They had to have someone on the spot to report whenever a new experiment had been carried out. Did he ever visit the Institute?'

'Yes. From time to time. I told you he was smashed up in Korea. Ebor treated him . . .'

'Yes. Ebor treated him. But he broke free at the end.'

'But what do they mean to do, Alan? They can't go on indefinitely with this. Someone will stumble on it, as we have.'

'No, I think the research and development phase is almost over now. I think they have got what they want. In fact I suspect that all this would have been dismantled in the very near future. As it is . . .'

'As it is, we've had to change our schedule slightly.'

We whirled as the door swung back. Standing there, the neon lighting harshly outlining them against the blackness. were Dorothy and Ramon. The Armillan wore a black polo-neck sweater and trousers; his companion, her dark hair scraped back as usual, was dressed in green ski-pants and jumper. Ramon held an automatic pistol pointing steadily halfway between us. Dorothy stood quietly beside him, her face solemn.

'Well, Alan, you seem to have survived our attempts to

take care of you.' Ramon's eyes were friendly, even merry. 'Korky told me you managed to send Gonzales over the cliff.' A speculative look appeared on his face. 'Would you mind telling me what kept you from jumping? Philip was sure you were one hundred per cent processed.'

I told him about Cygnus while my mind raced, calculated, squirrelled around in an effort to see a way out. I was conscious of the pistol in my right-hand trouser pocket; I was equally aware I had no chance of getting it out before he fired.

'Well, well,' he said. 'That was unfortunate. As it is, you've been quite a nuisance. And caused us to bring forward the day of departure.'

'For Armilla?' If I could only keep him talking.

Dorothy and Ramon exchanged glances.

'Ah, you've deduced that.'

Out of the corner of my eye I could see Jane's still profile.

'It was the logical answer to the question why. Your Armillan TV service will be something rather special, won't it? On the screens, in addition to westerns and soap operas and educational programmes there will be other, unscheduled educational programmes, simple, persuasive little sentences like "President O'Keefe is a good man", or "I am happy and contented in Armilla" or perhaps "I must tell the police if my neighbour speaks subversively". Unnoticed, of course, by the viewers but not without their soothing, controlling effects when applied night after night. And for those not convinced, those who rarely watch TV, a few psychedelic sessions like the ones I had can be arranged to reorientate their thinking.'

'But Philip . . .?' Jane spoke almost querulously.

'Philip is coming with us,' O'Keefe replied. 'He's done as much as he can accomplish here. In fact at present he's tidying up at the Institute.'

'But why? Why should he throw over everything like this?' Jane's puzzlement was obvious. 'He was carrying out really valuable work here. Why should he aid you in this—this police state control system?'

'It's because it is a police state,' I said gently. 'Ebor is obsessed with the desire to understand the human brain.

But in civilised nations, you cannot conduct experiments with people's brains. Sometimes there are opportunities, during necessary brain surgery, of learning a little more but for Ebor this is not enough, progress is frustratingly slow, he feels hampered. But,' I said slowly, 'I think his price for helping Ramon and his dear old dad to produce a nation of satisfied zombies is a free hand. Is that it, Ramon? What's a few disappearances among friends?'

Jane's lips parted in incredulous horror.

Ramon's grin was brittle. 'Philip believes that in five years of unrestricted experimentation with human subjects he can blueprint the human brain and understand for the first time mental processes. This he believes to be worth the price.'

Then God damn him to hell, I thought, my memory recalling simultaneously the animal laboratory Peter had shown me and Jerry Colombo's haunted face when he told me how he had searched for his girl.

'He can't get away with it,' Jane whispered. I watched Dorothy and wondered which one, Ramon or Ebor, she was involved with.

'He will,' Ramon promised. 'Two hours from now he and I and Dorothy will be outside British air space; by mid-morning we'll be safe in Armilla. Even if the British authorities learn about various sad events here and want us back, there will be no extradition from Armilla.' He smiled. 'How fortunate I brought a roll of tape with me. One never knows when one may have a use for anything, does one?' He dug his free hand in his trouser pocket, drew out a black ice-hockey puck of insulating tape and a penknife.

'Dorothy, would you mind taping our friends' hands and feet? Do Alan first. I think he'll behave.' He aimed the gun at Jane's head, two feet from her. I felt as if a tight steel band constrained my breathing. Two minutes later I was sitting on the hard concrete floor, feet taped together, my hands bound behind my back, a column of the Handiangle framework passing between my forearms. The tarry smell of the insulating tape was pungent in my fear-sensitised nostrils. In a sick rage I watched as Jane was forced to submit to the same treatment. During the six minutes, the only sound had been the occasional rasp as Dorothy tore free a new length of tape. At last she stood up. Ramon dropped the gun in his pocket and checked her work.

'Good. How much tape is left?'

She showed him. He cut four long strips, winding them tightly round our heads to form effective gags. He patted Jane's face.

'Sorry about this, darling. I would have liked to take you with me to Armilla as a souvenir. Once you had been re-educated you would have been most co-operative. As it is, however, I think it better that you and Alan are silenced without further delay.'

Dorothy stirred. 'You're going to shoot them now?'

Ramon hesitated then his face hardened. 'No. We'll make them sweat for a while before they go.' He left the hut, appearing after a few seconds carrying two large drums in his arms. He put them down with a gasp on the middle of the floor. He disappeared once more to return with a metal cylinder about a foot long and two inches in diameter. Holding it up like a field-marshal's baton, he said: 'This is something we had in case we were forced to leave in a hurry—as you have made us do. A thermite bomb, with a clockwork timing device. I set the timer, thus'—he screwed round the milled end—'for forty-five minutes from now, push over this switch to start it, so . . . you can stop it by pushing the switch back but of course that is academic where you are concerned—and that is that.' He took the rest of the insulating tape and taped the bomb to the television camera above my head.

'Oh yes,' he added, as if by afterthought, 'the drums contain jellied petrol, just to complete the job. In forty-five minutes from now, the bomb will explode, the temperature will rise to such a height that cold steel runs like water and no one will ever be able to make sense of the remains. Your friends Peter and Alison will doubtless be distressed by your disappearances—they might even connect them with Dorothy and Philip joining me in Armilla, but,' he shrugged, 'what can they prove?'

I wrinkled my brow in an attempt to stop sweat running into my eyes.

'We'll think of you. In fact we'll probably see blast-off.' He glanced at the television screen facing me. 'In the past six months we've become quite expert on programmes. This one beginning now lasts one hour including commercials. The bomb will explode ten minutes after the second commercial break ends. Are you sitting comfortably?' He glanced round the walls. 'All right, Dorothy, time we were moving.' He raised a hand. '*Hasta la vista.*'

They switched off the neon strip, pulled the door to and were gone. In the semi-darkness the figures on the luminous screen capered gaily. My eyes accommodated themselves to the palely gleaming frames and apparatus in their pools of black shadows. I swung my head left. A yard away, Jane's hazel eyes stared back, her brows raised, the crisscrossed tape blotting out her mouth. She raised her chin and I knew she was looking at the cylinder some three feet above my head. She arched her body, straining, twisting and I began to do likewise in an attempt to loosen the tape or move the framework.

We must have wasted ten minutes in this futile effort before, as if by mutual agreement, we collapsed back, breathing rapidly. I turned to Jane again. In her frenzied struggles her blue skirt and paler slip had been pushed back to the tops of her thighs, beyond the tops of her stockings. She glanced down, straightened her long legs, looked at me with widened, ironic eyes and shrugged. I had the incredible notion that behind the black gag she was smiling wryly. A turmoil of fury boiled inside me at my utter helplessness to free us, or to prevent Ramon and the others from getting away. The murderous rage shaking my body made me understand how a human being can go berserk. And then I froze.

On the TV screen a well-nourished farmer's wife, mouthing silently, smiling persuasively, offered us a slice of cheese, sampling it herself with nauseating gustatory enthusiasm. The brand name appeared at frequent intervals. She was followed by the other commercials in that break before the second part of the programme began. I felt my scalp crawl with the consciousness of the deadly little cylinder behind me ticking away our lives.

I found Jane's eyes on me. She flicked them to the left then tilted her head rapidly in that direction. I tried to decode the message. Fully five minutes passed before I got it, minutes during which the sheer agony she felt at her inability to convey what she wanted was balanced only by my angry frustration at my stupidity in reading the message.

From where she was it was impossible to reach the semi-transparent mirror clamped before the television receiver; in my position it was worth trying. In this situation, anything was worth trying. I twisted round so that I could bend my legs, still keeping them on the ground. Pulling them in under me, with the Handi-angle column biting into my back, I tried to get to my feet. I failed time and time again while Jane, absolutely motionless, stared at me, willing me to succeed. Finally, after an eternity, I managed to push myself up, my head hunching forward to escape the lens of the TV camera. The thought occurred to me that because my head now effectively eclipsed the screen, the houses in Port Mean using this channel would lose the programme. Normal service will be resumed as soon as possible, the idiot part of me quipped.

In front of me, at a height of about four feet, was the lower edge of the mirror. I gripped the L-shaped metal column and pressed my back against it, feeling my muscles creak. I breathed deeply, my body slippery with sweat, then brought both legs swinging up and out. At the third attempt I dislodged the sheet of glass from its clamp. It rose, twisting, then fell, just missing my dropping feet and shattered on the concrete, a number of the fragments reflecting the screen's pale light like shallow pools.

My breathing gusty, I released my grip and slid to the floor, legs outstretched. As fast as I dared I used my heels to drag a large fragment to me. Twisting my body, I slid the long glass shard behind me and into my hands. I dropped it once in trying to arrange it and scrabbled for it in a muck sweat. Finally I managed to slide it into one of the slots in the column, clamping it by pushing my body against it sideways so that I could feel its edge through jacket and shirt. I now began to saw the tape around my wrists.

A minute passed, two. I was utterly incapable, except by touch, of judging what progress I was making. Cramp began to seize me but I kept my position for fear of dislodging the glass knife or breaking it off. I felt the tapes give a little.

The second commercial break began. I forced myself to continue at the same methodical pace while my memory supplied the jingle to the film clip of a man playing darts in a pub. Almost anything you do, goes-a-little-better when you chew, Wrigley's spearmint gum. Maybe I should have bought a packet. The tape ripped and I jerked my hands apart.

Sawing my ankles free took twenty seconds. I stood up, whirling round towards the cylinder as the last part of the programme appeared. Ramon had taped the cylinder so that the switch was on the inside. I hoped fervently his maths and his device were both accurate. I sawed away the tape until I could prise the cylinder free. Holding it to my ear I heard the devilish little cricket tick-tick-tick. Pushing the switch back, I listened again. It was now silent. By my reckoning, count-down had been held at T minus 5.

I ripped the tarry tape off my lips in two quick stinging tugs and turned to Jane. When I finally drew her to her feet she clung to me. I held her until the brief storm of weeping passed and kissed her wet face.

'We have to go now, Jane. There may still be a chance to stop them.'

She looked up at me, her eyes shadowed. Then her mouth tightened and she had herself under control once more. When we left the concrete hut, the trees were black columns against the twilight sky. During the walk through the wood, I felt drained, tired as if I hadn't slept for a week, but my mind raced, trying to predict the route Ramon and the others would take and how we could intercept them.

15 Death's bright beacon

The car was untouched. We tumbled in and sat with all lights out.

'What can we do?' Jane asked. 'Go to the police?'

'Not enough time.'

'But we have evidence now.'

'Oh yes, we could convince them—eventually. But how many hours would pass before they set the wheels turning?'

'I suppose so.'

'Look, Jane, what did Ramon say exactly?'

'He said that in two hours' time they would be outside British air space. And by mid-morning they'd be safe in Armilla. They must be flying out.'

'Yes. But there aren't any commercial night flights from Machrihanish. It closes down. The local Islay-Campbeltown-Glasgow run is by day only. So they can't get to Glasgow before mid-day tomorrow that way.'

'A helicopter. Supposing they landed one and got to the mainland that way.'

'It's possible. Or they could go round by road. It'd take a fast car about four hours, no more. But there can't be direct flights from Glasgow or Prestwick to Armilla. They'd still have to break their journey, probably at New York. They might even have to fly to Havana from London and go on from there. I just can't see them getting home by mid-morning that way. And in any case I imagine they'll have lots of luggage they'll want to keep from Customs inspection: files, maybe apparatus, data. And remember. This journey was forced on them by my actions. They hadn't a great deal of time to plan this or book reservations.'

'Do you think Ramon was lying, then?'

'No. He had no need to.' I knuckled my forehead. 'Two hours. And in Armilla by mid-morning.' Something in the back of my mind dodged scrutiny. I pressed the side of my forefinger against my teeth. And then I had it.

'Jane! Get the car on to the main road for Campbeltown. Quick! I'll explain as we go.'

She fired the engine, switched on headlamps whose light was splashed back harshly from surrounding bushes, and reversed the Imp out, its engine whining. She turned it and aimed for the drive entrance. A minute later we were racing down the hill towards Carskiey and the Lephenstrath Bridge while I checked my argument again.

'I think they're flying direct from Machrihanish tonight.'

Jane's head whipped round momentarily.

'But that's impossible!'

'No. There's one way.' I told her about the news item I'd read at Borgadel House the Sunday afternoon she'd come to collect me, how the President's plane had narrowly escaped damage from a falling bomb. 'That plane's a modified Tupolev Tu-114. It's based on the Russian Tu-20 Bear strategic bomber. When the direct service between Moscow and Havana was started, about 1963, Tu-114s were used. They're huge planes, four-engined turbo-props with a fantastic range. That plane of Ramon's father could, with absolutely minimum payload, possibly with auxiliary fuel-tanks, do much more than 6,000 miles. And you can be sure it's always kept in a state of readiness with a completely trustworthy crew in case the President has to depart suddenly with a few financial souvenirs.'

'You mean it could actually take-off from Armilla, land here, pick them up without refuelling and get back?'

'Yes.' The car swung sharp left at South Carrine, its tyres screeching.

'But Machrihanish Airport is surely far too small to take it.'

'I don't know. I wish to God I'd taken more notice of it the couple of times I've come down by air.'

'But surely you just can't land a huge plane like that on any airport when you feel like it, even if the runway is long enough and the place shuts down at night. In any case, Alan, Machrihanish is Royal Air Force as well as civil. And what about radar surveillance? They'd be picked up well out in the Atlantic.'

I was silent while the Imp bucketed along until Jane braked, swung sharp left again and accelerated on the main road past Keprigan. When she levelled off, the Imp must have been doing seventy.

'I'm not so sure. If they came in below 500 feet for the last stages of their flight I'd guess they'd escape radar until they were quite close to the coast. It'd be damn risky but with a good pilot and good visibility it'd work. And before that? They *might* be seen. But if they were, inertia and the complicated and crowded pattern of Atlantic air traffic would help them. If they chose a commercial route, they'd be taken first of all for an unscheduled commercial flight—after a time-consuming search had been made among records. Or possibly a military flight; again a search and identify operation would be needed with a great deal of to-ing and fro-ing calls among heaven knows how many people. I think time would be on their side. And then, at the last moment, they take a new course having come down to 500 feet.'

I grimaced. 'The landing is the dodgy part in more ways than one. Presumably the pilot hasn't landed anything here before. His navigator will have to pick up the navigation beacons in the neighbourhood. Yes!' I suddenly remembered the study we'd made of possible sources of radio noise in the vicinity of the Outstation when we were planning to put up the forty-five foot radio dish. 'There's the Kintyre radio beacon, always operational. And the Skipness beacon and visual omnirange, also the Machrihanish visual omnirange. In the aircraft they'd have a loop aerial to give them direction. And if the sky is clear'—I looked out—'and it seems to be—the moon's almost full—the pilot can be guided in to where local coastal features can tie him in to make his final approach. I imagine he'll come in from the sea.' I shook my head. 'Oh, there are all sorts of difficulties. Landing lights? R.A.F. personnel to cope with? Appearance on radar during the final approach?'

I suddenly felt doubtful. 'And yet, nothing else makes sense. When they decided to pull out this morning they must have sent a pre-arranged code signal by radio via the Armillan Embassy to get that Tu-114 on its way. That aircraft must be coming in over the western Atlantic right now, only three aircraft lengths above the waves.'

'But what about the final approach? They'd be picked up on the local radar. Even five minutes' warning would surely be enough to enable the base people to get jeeps and trucks on to the runway.'

'Yes, that's the weak point.' I thought for a moment. 'They've got to cut down that warning time to the absolute minimum. Ebor can't count on knocking out the radar by cutting off power. Even if he were ambitious enough to seek out and sever the power lines, a station like Machrihanish could well have its own emergency supply.'

A car coming the other way neglected to dip its headlights. I looked away, blinded by the brilliant dazzle of light.

'Idiot,' I muttered, then gasped. 'That's it. That's how it can be done. Don't knock out the radar. Blind it.' My brain raced. 'Supposing Ebor rigged up a portable transmitter on the radar frequencies—he could do it—got one of Ramon's men to take it in a motorboat some miles out to sea, and at the right moment simply sprayed interference in the land direction. He could even add verisimilitude by sending out a Mayday call before he made his radio act up. If the RAF thought the faulty radio was in a boat in distress a few miles out they'd probably send out their air sea rescue launch, but I doubt if they would immediately alert their air traffic control people. And the Tupolev would come in unseen. The first sign of its presence would be the noise of its engines. By the time they were heard clearly enough to give a direction, the plane would be making its final approach. And at two hundred knots it'd be down practically before they realised it was going to land.'

I laughed shortly. 'You know, in the darkness, it's not all that different in appearance to a Boeing 707. That'd help to make them hesitate before hitting the panic button.'

'Can't we inform the RAF people?'

'I doubt if there's time. It's the same problem as the police. In any case,' I added wryly, 'can you see us driving up to the station gatehouse and saying to the Security Officer: "Thought you should know, old man, that a Russian Tupolev Tu-114 will be landing in two minutes. Please arrange for its reception." ' I paused. 'No, it's up to us.'

'But what can we do? They're armed.'

'So are we.' I touched my trouser pocket. 'I've still got Korky's gun.'

'But can you use it?'

'Oh yes. I've done a fair amount of hunting in the States. And,' I added hesitantly, 'I used to go with a girl in Maryland whose father was mad-keen on pistol-shooting. President of the local gun club. I—uh—used to practice with him, to be sociable, you know.'

She gave me a quick glance, her eyes glinting, her mouth twitching, before she studied the road again. I wished I felt as confident as I sounded.

'Turn left at Stewarton,' I said. I remembered that on the day of my accident I had bypassed Campbeltown by turning westwards three miles northwest of the town along the road crossing the Mull, then driving south by the narrow single track over the Aros Moss. The road crosses a wide stretch of low-lying boggy saltflats covered with coarse grass and clumps of bushes that forms the Mull of Kintyre's waist. In no place is the track more than fifty feet above sea level; at one point it passes within thirty yards of the west end of the runway where there is no perimeter fence. At that time of night there would be no traffic along it.

The Imp slowed and turned left. A third of a mile along the Machrihanish road we turned north on to the lonely

Aros Moss road. Jane switched off the headlights. Through the windscreen about three and a half miles to the north-west I could see a few lights from the RAF camp a mile beyond the runway. Friday night. Probably half of them would be away on 'forty-eights'.

The moon was dim behind thin cloud and the line of steep hills crossing the Mull to the north showed black against the lighter sky. Two miles eastwards the lights of Campbeltown were mostly hidden behind gentler, lower hills. We crossed the Machrihanish water, took the right fork between hedgerows and I told Jane to kill the side-lights. At ten miles an hour we covered a further four hundred yards before we stopped. She switched off the engine. In the car darkness was complete. Outside, nearby bushes, the hedges on either side, could be seen dimly and the sky-line was clear but beyond fifty yards everything merged in blackness.

'I'll go on foot now,' I said. 'It's less than half a mile from here to the runway end. That's where they'll be.'

I broke off. Almost at the limit of audibility but unmistakably there, the faraway sound of an aircraft's engines touched the utter silence. I opened my door wide. The whispery throb strengthened.

'That's it! It'll come straight in, turn at this end, pick them up and take-off seawards. Inertia's in their favour. By the time the RAF gets anyone airborne—from Leuchars, say, they'll be outside British airspace. There's no time for anything fancy. I'll try to hold them. If I delay the plane's take-off long enough, the RAF base people will have trucks and fire engines round it.'

'I'm coming with you . . .'

'No. Give me five minutes exactly then switch on, headlights as well, and drive through to the base. Drive like hell. By the time you get there they'll have realised something's up. You'll be able to guide their efforts to discover what's happening.'

I closed the door and began trotting along the track, the gun in my right hand. The moon came out and visibility improved. I began to sprint, trying with long shallow steps to keep as quiet as possible. On both sides the Moss spread out, grass blotched with the shadows of bushes or slashed by the black lines of irrigation ditches. Low rises to the west hid the sea. The aircraft was much closer now, its engines droning insistently. My breath quickened and I wondered how many minutes had passed. I approached a corner, halted and peered round the ragged edge. And there they were.

They had drawn a small van off the narrow track. Twenty yards further on, the runway began, stretching palely to the western horizon, its edges angled by perspective, the moonlight transforming its concrete surface to ice, as if it were a frozen extension of the ocean beyond. It was long. I wondered if it was long enough.

Three figures stood ahead of the van on the runway end, sooty smudges on its surface. They faced westwards expectantly.

The aircraft was still invisible but couldn't be more than four miles out, judging by the dull roar. If it was doing about two hundred knots it'd be on us in just over a minute. Suddenly four lights flared skywards, like miniature searchlights, one at each corner of this end of the runway, two more, fainter, at the seaward end. Ebor must have sent someone—one of Ramon's men?—along the runway to set up improvised lights. On such a clear night, at the height of summer, four accident handlamps with powerful batteries would be all that was required. I saw a moving speck at the far end of the runway and realised it was a car speeding back towards us along the runway edge. Ramon's man didn't intend to be left behind.

I sprinted forward to the van, keeping it between me and Ebor's group. There was no one in the driving seat. In the darkness, I pulled the door open, hope flaring briefly. But the key wasn't in the lock. As I expected, the back was crammed with cases and crates. The sound of the plane's engines was a shrill scream when I backed out and began to run towards the group. The Tu-114 was visible now, making its final approach, a black ruler with a blob in the middle dropping down between the goalposts of lights at the far end. In the RAF base houses a mile away, more lights began to appear.

The pilot was first-rate. As far as I could see, he put the massive plane down on the extreme end of the runway, almost immediately applying full reverse thrust to shorten his run. The three would-be passengers were still watching the shrieking aircraft's approach when I stopped six feet behind them. I had to shout to be heard.

'Turn round! And put your hands up!'

Ramon swung round first. His face contorted into a mixture of horror, disbelief and fury. The others sensed his movement, turned. Ebor's hawk-like face flinched before he darted an accusing glance at his companions. Dorothy gave a little cry, her features crumpled, and she hid her face in her hands. The Tu-114 was less than half a mile away, decelerating fast. The noise from the four huge turbo-props was already deafening.

I meant to order them away from the van, over past the end of the runway and make them lie prone, the better to control them. But Ramon was too quick. He threw himself flat behind the others, trying to get his own gun out. I swung my pistol, hesitated, irrationally hoping to avoid his two companions. Ebor and Dorothy froze. I got a glimpse of Ramon, overcame my instincts and fired. Flame flared from his gun. The bullet passed over my shoulder. Ebor darted out of the line of fire, dragging Dorothy with him. I suddenly saw that the other car had stopped fifty yards away, the door was open and a man was on the tarmac, sprinting towards us, something in his hand. The approaching plane's engines completely killed the sound of the gunfire.

I saw that I was within three yards of the waist-high grass and bushes at the edge of the runway. Ramon fired again as I dodged sideways; the other man stopped, straddle-legged, aimed at me and I jumped into the undergrowth, falling flat. Both men fired as I wriggled deeper in. I turned over, pressed the trigger twice and changed position fast. Judging by the number of bullets zipping through the bushes, Ebor must have joined in. Faintly, through the nerve-searing shriek of the transport's power plants, I heard a siren rise to a high-pitched wail.

I peered cautiously above the tall grass. Ramon and his

man stood twenty yards away, guns in hand, watching for me. Ebor and Dorothy had disappeared but were presumably in the van for it began to move, bumping on to the tarmac. A hurricane of wind suddenly beat me flat as the Tu-114, looming blackly over everyone, swung slowly round, the tip of its great sweptback port wing actually passing far above my head. It halted, facing seawards, its engines screaming impatiently. The noise was excruciating on the nervous system, bringing tears to my eyes, bludgeoning any thoughts I had.

The van ran behind the huge wheels, forty feet apart, and stopped. Ramon and his man broke and ran. Any idea I'd had of approaching I dismissed when five denim-clad men swung down a ladder on the far side and spread out under the plane, sub-machine-guns cradled in their arms, ready to deal with any opposition. All I could do was watch while others attached hooks on cables to the van and it was hoisted upwards out of sight. The men swarmed up the ladder after it, the guards turned and followed them. Within thirty seconds of the plane's arrival, it was ready to move. The turboprops' scream intensified as they climbed to full thrust, the brakes were released and with hands pressed over my tortured ears, I sat, buffeted by a fresh hurricane, watching the Tu-114 hurl itself down the runway, accelerating to achieve lift-off velocity before it reached the sea end. Along the roads connecting the long concrete apron with the RAF quarters, trucks raced, two carrying searchlights; men ran, the siren still shrieked and the houses blazed with light but the Tupolev was now a mile down the runway.

I stood up, utterly exhausted, feeling chilled to the marrow. A figure ran to meet me from a parked car, its headlights blazing. It was Jane. She gripped my arms, the moonlight white on her taut, strained face.

'Are you all right?'

I slid my arm round her shoulder.

'Yes. Didn't you get through?'

'I couldn't make myself go on.' She sobbed once, staring down the pale runway at the fleeing aircraft. 'They got away! We couldn't stop them.'

The pilot achieved lift-off speed. The spinning wheels rose and the four raging power plants raised the giant plane out over the water with a dull roar like cannon balls rolling down a metal floor. In the warm, well-lit spacious passenger compartment, Ebor, Ramon and Dorothy would still be tense, a trifle anxious but in general in a state of understandable euphoria at their escape. Even if the Tu-114 were chased, they couldn't be made to turn back now. I thought of Korky, of Innes Carr, of the young girl who had committed suicide in Port Mean, of Ramon's attempt to kill Jane and myself, of the unhallowed future plans of Ebor and Ramon in Armilla. I paid no attention to the whining trucks approaching us along the runway; my eyes were riveted on the shrinking Tu-114.

It came when the aircraft was almost out of sight, a black toy against the dark blue western sky. From the centre of the fuselage a bright scarlet rose blossomed and I imagined the dark hills lightened momentarily in sympathy. A blazing inferno, the Tu-114 ceased its upward climb and began its steep parabolic dive to extinction in the Atlantic's grey waters. Twenty seconds later, as the first jeep skidded to a halt beside us, the rumble of the explosion reached our ears.

I looked down at Jane's stunned face and wondered if I could ever tell her, or she would ever guess, that I had brought from the repeater station Ramon's thermite cylinder, or that I had slid it into Ebor's brief-case in the van after pushing over the switch. As Ramon himself had remarked, one never knows when one may have a use for anything.

DEADLIGHT

Is there any connection between the chilling discovery made by John Marshall, research scientist of Glasgow University's Department of Cybernetic Studies and his inexplicable death shortly afterwards on the Island of Arran? His widow thinks so and persuades their friend Roger Arran, who knows the island well, to overcome his reluctance to visit its shores again.

What he finds not only involves him in violence and danger on the soaring mountains of the island but leads him, once he has solved the mystery of the Tormore Circles and the Slaughter Stone, to a secret so powerful that it must change the future of mankind.

ALL EVIL SHED AWAY

The island of St Kilda, that mysterious, storm-bound outpost of the Outer Hebrides of Scotland, was evacuated in 1930 and left to the sea and its wildlife. Now it is the closely-guarded place to which research scientist David Hamilton finds himself taken – ostensibly to aid in the development of an intriguing, top-secret project.

Very soon, however, he is forced to realise that the part he is destined to play is specially hazardous, involving him in decisions affecting the lifes of many, including his own, and pitting him against the most evil regime ever recorded in history.

Apogee Books may be ordered from the following address: Apogee Books, P.O. Box 230, Glasgow G12 9EX, United Kingdom

Please send cheque or postal order (no currency) and allow 55p for postage and packing for the first book plus 22p for the second book and 14p for each additional book ordered.

Customers in Eire and B.F.P.O. please allow 55p for the first book, 22p for the second book and 14p per copy for the next 7 books, thereafter 8p per book.

Overseas customers please allow £1.00 for postage and packing for the first book and 25p per copy for each additional book.

Titles of books by Archie Roy published in the present series by Apogee Books

The Curtained Sleep	ISBN 1 869935 00 4
Deadlight	ISBN 1 869935 01 2
All Evil Shed Away	ISBN 1 869935 02 0